ALEX MORGAN

Simon & Schuster Books for Young Readers
New York   London   Toronto   Sydney   New Delhi

SIMON & SCHUSTER BOOKS FOR YOUNG READERS

An imprint of Simon & Schuster Children's Publishing Division

1230 Avenue of the Americas, New York, New York 10020

This book is a work of fiction. Any references to historical events, real people,
or real places are used fictitiously. Other names, characters, places, and events are products
of the author's imagination, and any resemblance to actual events or places or
persons, living or dead, is entirely coincidental.

Text copyright © 2014 by Alex Morgan and Full Fathom Five

Cover illustration copyright © 2014 by Paula Franco

SIMON & SCHUSTER BOOKS FOR YOUNG READERS is a trademark of Simon & Schuster, Inc.

For information about special discounts for bulk purchases, please contact Simon &
Schuster Special Sales at 1-866-506-1949 or business@simonandschuster.com.

The Simon & Schuster Speakers Bureau can bring authors to your live event. For more
information or to book an event, contact the Simon & Schuster Speakers Bureau at
1-866-248-3049 or visit our website at www.simonspeakers.com.

Also available in a Simon & Schuster Books for Young Readers hardcover edition

Book design by Krista Vossen

The text for this book is set in Berling.

Manufactured in the United States of America

0715 OFF

First Simon & Schuster Books for Young Readers paperback edition August 2014

6 8 10 9 7 5

The Library of Congress has cataloged the hardcover edition as follows:

Morgan, Alex (Alexandra Patricia), 1989–

Win or lose / Alex Morgan. — First edition.

pages cm. — (The Kicks ; [3])

Summary: "Devin's team thinks she is taking too much credit for their winning
streak and she must keep the team together"— Provided by publisher.

ISBN 978-1-4424-8580-8 (hardback) — ISBN 978-1-4424-8584-6 (ebook)

ISBN 978-1-4424-8582-2 (pbk)

[1. Soccer—Fiction. 2. Friendship—Fiction. 3. Teamwork (Sports)—Fiction.
4. Family life—California—Fiction. 5. California—Fiction.] I. Title.

PZ7.M818Win 2014 [Fic]—dc23

2013022773

FOR ALL U.S. WOMEN'S SOCCER FANS
FOR THEIR CONTINUED SUPPORT
AS WE EMBARK ON OUR JOURNEY
TO BRING THE WORLD CUP HOME.
LIVE CONFIDENTLY.
FOLLOW YOUR DREAMS.

CHAPTER ONE

"Stay on your toes! You gotta be ready for the ball!" Coach Flores shouted encouragingly.

I stood across from my friend Jessi at soccer practice at Kentville Middle School, a soccer ball in my hands. I tossed the ball to her. Jessi stopped it with her upper thigh, bounced it down to her foot, and kicked it back at me. We were doing a volley exercise, passing the ball back and forth using different parts of our body.

"Keep it coming, Devin!" Jessi called out as she danced around on her feet, waiting for the ball.

I threw the ball again, and this time Jessi ducked into it, her braids flapping in the wind as she hit the ball back to me with her head.

"Now, that's using your head!" my other friend Emma called to us, laughing at her own silly joke.

"Boo!" I heard Grace, the eighth-grade captain of the

Kentville Kangaroos (otherwise known as the Kicks), call out. "That's the oldest soccer joke in the book!"

"Not the oldest," Emma said with a gleam in her eyes. "Why did Cinderella get kicked off the soccer team?"

Groans broke out over the entire soccer field before all the Kicks replied together:

"Because she ran away from the ball!"

"Now, that," Emma said, smiling triumphantly, "is the oldest soccer joke around!"

Everyone started cracking up, even Coach, who chuckled as she glanced at her wristwatch. "We might as well call it quits. I haven't had a chance to check out today's paper, and I'd like to do that while you are all still here. The article about the Kicks was supposed to run today!"

Everyone began buzzing excitedly as Coach went to her office to get the newspaper.

"Do you think my photo is in it? I hope they got my good side!" said my friend Frida. (She wanted to be an actress someday, so she was always worried about her good side.)

"I have to text my mom and make sure she picks up a paper," Zoe added.

I grinned at my friends. When I'd first joined the Kicks at the start of the school year, the team hadn't been doing so well. But now we were headed to the play-offs, and a reporter and a photographer from the *Kentville Chronicle* had showed up at a practice the week before. The reporter had asked us a bunch of questions, and then the photographer had clicked away as we'd played a scrimmage.

"We're in luck! Coach Valentine left a bunch of copies on my desk," said Coach Flores. She gave one to Frida before she moved down the field, handing out newspapers randomly to the other Kicks as she went. Jessi, Emma, and Zoe huddled around Frida, and I joined them.

"It's in the sports section, section C," Coach called.

Frida eagerly leafed through the newspaper, dropping pages onto the field until she found the article.

"Ta-da!" she cried, pointing to the team photo of the Kicks plastered across the page. "Maybe a big casting director will see me in this photo and just have to have me in her next project!" She got a faraway look in her eyes.

"Um, hello?" Jessi said impatiently as she picked up the newspaper pages Frida had scattered all over the field. She straightened up and waved the pages in front of Frida's face. "We want to read the article!"

"Yeah!" Emma cried. "This is so exciting!"

I looked over Frida's shoulder and saw my teammates' smiling faces looking back at me from the newspaper. We all wore the blue-and-white Kentville uniforms, which we had worn especially for the photographer that day. I saw myself grinning, wearing—of course—my pink headband.

"Kentville Kangaroos 'Kick' Their Way to the Play-Offs . . ." Frida began to read the article as Emma clapped her hands excitedly.

"It's been more than twenty years since the Kentville

Kangaroos earned their nickname, 'the Kicks.' Coach Maria Luisa Flores should know," Frida continued reading aloud. "She was a member of the middle school soccer team when the Kangaroos were two-time state champs in 1991 and 1992. It was during this time that the team got their nickname for the arsenal of kicks they used against their opponents. The name 'the Kicks' might have stuck, but the team's winning streak didn't. The Kicks haven't seen a play-off season since 1996. Even when Flores came back to her hometown to coach for Kentville a couple of years ago, the team continued to struggle, finishing 10–1 last season. 'I was focused on fun and making it a positive experience for the girls,' Flores said about her early years as the Kangaroos' girls' coach. 'But the girls made it very clear to me that they wanted to have fun while being serious competitors at the same time.'"

"Losing all the time was *so* not fun!" Emma interrupted, and everyone nodded their agreement. Even though it had been only a few months ago, it seemed more like a lifetime ago when our practices had been basically chaotic messes.

I shuddered. "Do you remember how disorganized everything was?"

"What about the Panthers game when I scored in our own goal?" Emma asked. "You can't get any more disorganized than that!"

Coach's emphasis on fun and fair above all else hadn't worked out too well. When she'd combined it with solid coaching skills, the Kicks had finally started improving.

Frida continued reading: "Flores's new coaching attitude, and some fresh blood, turned the team around. A talented group of seventh graders, including Connecticut transplant Devin Burke, the seventh-grade co-captain, are widely regarded as having jump-started the team this season."

"Devin Burke! I know her!" Jessi yelled, jumping up and down. "Will you sign an autograph for me?"

I blushed. "Cut it out," I said, swatting her hands away as she tried to hug me, acting like a crazed fan. I felt totally weird that the newspaper was singling me out. We were a team! Before I could say anything else, Frida kept on reading:

"'I don't know where my team would be without me,' Burke said at practice. The team is gearing up for their first play-off match against the Newton Tigers this Saturday."

Frida's voice trailed off as the quote sank in. She stopped reading and looked at me, her mouth open. Jessi, Emma, and Zoe all stared at me too, with surprised—and hurt—looks in their eyes.

"Wow, Devin," Jessi said slowly. The joking smile from a moment ago left her face.

I don't know where my team would be without me. The sentence echoed in my head, over and over. It sounded so stuck-up.

"I never said that!" I cried, feeling like I was on trial, with their angry eyes staring at me. I thought back to the day when the reporter, Cassidy Vale, had visited our team.

She had seemed really interested in talking to me, especially after finding out I was not only new to the team but new to Kentville Middle School.

"And you were made co-captain?" she had asked with a raised eyebrow.

"Yes," I'd said, nodding, but I hadn't told her that part of the reason was that nobody else in the seventh grade had wanted to be a co-captain at the time. The team's disorganization, plus the fact that mean Mirabelle had been the eighth-grade captain, had made the job less than desirable.

But I knew I'd made sure to tell her how much being on the Kicks meant to me. She must have gotten my words mixed up.

"I swear! I told the reporter, 'I don't know where I would be without my team' not 'I don't know where my team would be without me.' You've got to believe me!" I felt like I had swallowed a rock and that it was slowly turning around and around in my stomach.

Emma gave me a sympathetic smile. "What was in the newspaper, it really doesn't sound like something you would say, Devin."

"Never!" I said. "I remember telling the reporter that 'I don't know where I would be without my team,' because I really don't! I was so scared on the first day of school. Meeting you guys and joining the Kicks was the best thing that could have happened. If I hadn't, I'd probably still be hiding out in the bathroom during lunch!" I gave a little hiccup as I choked back tears.

"Hey, Devin, relax," Jessi said slowly as she put her arm around me. "It just took us by surprise, that's all. And the reason it was so shocking is because we would never expect you to say something like that, never!"

"They misquoted you!" Frida said. "It happens to actors all the time. It's part of being in the public eye."

"All I want to do is play soccer, not be in the public eye and get all misquoted and stuff!" I felt miserable.

Zoe gave me a hug. "I believe you, Devin. Don't worry about it. Anyone who knows you would know you'd never say anything like that."

I was taller than Zoe, so as I hugged her back, I looked over her short strawberry-blond hair at Jessi, Emma, and Frida. They were all smiling at me.

"Group hug!" Jessi called. Zoe and I each opened an arm, and everyone came pouring in.

"Thanks, guys," I said, hugging them tight. "I don't know where I would be without my friends, and you can quote me on that!"

After we all untangled from our group hug, Jessi smiled up at me. "Let's focus on the positive, which is that the Kicks have made it to play-offs!"

"Yes!" I pumped a fist in the air. "And we all worked together as a team to make that happen."

Zoe looked up. "My dad's here. Time to go!"

I followed her gaze to the parking lot next to the field. It was filling up with cars, as practice was supposed to be done by now. I spotted my family's white minivan.

Maisie, my little sister, called it the Marshmallow.

We walked over to the benches to grab our stuff, and as we did, I noticed the other Kicks still huddled around newspapers in groups. For a second I'd forgotten that the entire team was reading the article. What were they thinking about me?

We walked by Grace, the eighth-grade co-captain. She was talking with Anjali, Maya, and Giselle, all eighth graders. They looked up at us as we passed, giving me a dirty look. I stopped in my tracks.

"Look, guys, about the article," I began.

"Yeah, about the article," Anjali said. "Thanks for being on our team, Devin. I don't know what we'd do without you." Her voice dripped with sarcasm. Maya and Giselle giggled, but Grace just looked at me intently.

"That was a pretty rude thing to say," she said quietly.

"I didn't say it! I swear!" I felt like I was back at square one. I explained what I had really said and how I'd been misquoted.

"Okay, Devin," Grace said. But I could tell she didn't believe me.

"Are we cool?" I asked.

She nodded curtly but didn't say anything. Uh-oh. I didn't think we were cool at all. More like ice cold, actually.

As I went to catch up with my friends, I saw Alandra, Taylor, and Zarine join Grace and her friends. They were all eighth graders too. Anjali started whispering loudly, nodding in my direction from time to time. I heard the other girls whispering back to her as they shot looks at me.

I felt my shoulders slump as I walked to the parking lot. My best friends believed me, but it was pretty obvious my other teammates didn't.

CHAPTER TWO

Mom noticed my face as soon as I climbed into the seat next to her.

"Devin, what's wrong?" she asked.

I put a copy of the newspaper on her lap. "Remember that reporter who came last week? Well, she misquoted me, and now everyone's mad at me." I explained to her about what it said in the article.

Mom frowned. "That's terrible, Devin. As soon as we get home, we'll contact the newspaper and ask for a correction."

"But you *are* the best on the team," my little sister Maisie piped up from the backseat.

I sighed. "Thanks, Maisie. But that's not really true. We've got a lot of strong players. The whole point is that we won because we're a strong team. That's what I was trying to say."

"I'm sure your teammates will understand it, once

they've had time to think about it," Mom said, but I wasn't so sure.

When we got to the house, Mom turned on the laptop that was in our kitchen, and we looked up the newspaper. It was too late to call, but there was a link to e-mail Cassidy Vale.

"Do you want me to write this?" Mom asked, but I shook my head.

"No, I got this," I told her. I sat down at the table and started to type. I'd been thinking of what I wanted to say during the whole ride home.

Dear Ms. Vale,

Please make a correction to the article you wrote about the Kentville Kangaroos. I never said, "I don't know where my team would be without me." I said, "I don't know where I would be without my team." My team-mates are upset, so please make the correction.

Thanks,
Devin Burke

I felt relieved when I hit send. Problem solved, right? Feeling better, I clicked on my MyBook page. Taylor had made a post right at the top of my page:

You're not here, Devin, so I don't know where I am! :-p

I felt that rock in my stomach again. I thought about typing something in response, but I just deleted Taylor's post instead. Then I sent her a private message.

> Taylor, you have to believe me! I never said that. I e-mailed
> the reporter, and the paper is going to run a correction.

I sent the message, and then I checked to see if Taylor was online. She was, and I figured she'd respond right away, but she didn't. Then I noticed that some of my seventh-grade soccer friends were online: Brianna, Sarah, and Anna. I hadn't gotten a chance to talk to them after practice, and I wanted to know if they were mad too. So I started a chat.

> Wanted to say I'm sorry about that newspaper article.
> I would never say anything like that. The reporter got it
> wrong. I hope you're not mad.

A reply from Brianna popped up quickly: That didn't sound like you.

Then Sarah joined in: Not mad! ☺

Then Anna: Not mad ethr. But 8th graders are talking. ☹

Thanks, I replied. I know.

"Devin, can you please shut down the laptop and set the table?" Mom asked.

"Sure," I said. I didn't have the heart to stay online anyway. I had a feeling that things might get worse.

• • •

The next day was gloomy and rainy, which was not something I was used to seeing in Southern California. It was almost always sunny. But at least the weather matched my mood.

"I wonder if we'll have practice today," I said as I pushed around my salad with my fork. Usually I ate lunch outside with my friends in the library courtyard, but because of the rain we were sitting inside the noisy cafeteria instead.

"I doubt it," Jessi said. She was busy pulling the crust off the tuna sandwich her mom had packed for her.

I usually hated having to miss a practice, but today I felt almost relieved. I knew a bunch of the eighth graders were still mad about yesterday's newspaper article.

I let out a big sigh. Emma noticed. "What's wrong, Devin?" she asked as she looked up from her orange-and-pink bento box. It was a lunch box with little compartments inside to keep the food separate.

"It's the eighth graders," I began, and then I explained about what Taylor had written on my wall.

Jessi's jaw dropped. "Rude!"

"I took it down right away," I said. "And I private messaged her, trying again to explain what really happened. But she wouldn't answer me. I don't get it. My seventh-grade friends believe me. I don't know why the eighth graders won't!" I pushed my salad away and plunked my head down onto the table, miserable.

"They'll get over it," Jessi said confidently. "Don't worry."

"I hope you're right," I mumbled, my forehead still resting on the table.

"Just give them a couple of days," Emma said. "It will blow over."

Emma was right. I just needed to be patient. Everything would go back to normal. After all, we were a team. I lifted my head up and began to eat some of the crispy chicken salad I had gotten from the cafeteria, feeling a little bit better. I'd been so distracted this morning that I'd forgotten my lunch.

"I, for one, will be glad if practice gets canceled," Zoe said as she took out a huge binder from her book bag. Bits of colored papers and ribbons were hanging out of it.

"Whoa!" Jessi cried. "That binder looks like it ate all of my notebooks for breakfast!"

Frida had been busy writing in her own notebook, doing some last-minute homework. Her eyes grew wide as she hugged her notebook to her, pretending to be scared of Zoe's binder. "Don't worry. I won't let anything happen to you," she whispered to her notebook, and we all cracked up.

"It's my party planning book," Zoe said defensively. "Remember? For my bat mitzvah? I've got lots to do, so if we don't have practice today, I'll use the extra time to finalize some of my plans."

For a second we all had blank looks on our faces.

"Don't tell me you forgot!" Zoe shrieked. "We're all supposed to go look for dresses tomorrow!"

Jessi and I exchanged glances. With all the excitement

of making play-offs, and then the newspaper article yesterday, I had completely forgotten all about dress shopping with Zoe. I could tell from the grimace on Jessi's face that she hadn't remembered either.

"Of course we didn't forget, Zoe." Emma shot us a warning glance as she said this. "It's just been hectic with play-offs and everything."

Zoe sighed. "Tell me about it. I never would have guessed in a million years at the start of the season that the Kicks would be in the play-offs. I thought I'd have plenty of time to plan the party. It has to be perfect, just like all of my sisters' bat mitzvahs were."

Zoe was the youngest of four sisters. You could totally tell they were related, because they looked so much alike. They were all petite with the same strawberry-blond hair, and all of them, Zoe included, dressed like they'd just stepped out of a magazine. Today Zoe was wearing a pink-and-white striped top under a floral print blazer. Since Zoe put such care and attention into what she wore every day, I wasn't surprised that she'd put that same effort into planning her party.

"You know I'm super-excited about your bat mitzvah, Zoe," I told her. "I've never been to one before!"

When Zoe had invited me, she'd explained that a bat mitzvah was a Jewish religious ceremony. "When a girl turns thirteen, she is considered an adult under Jewish law," Zoe had told me. "There's a ceremony first, and then a huge party to celebrate!"

Zoe smiled now. "I'm glad you feel that way, Devin. Because I was looking at the play-off schedule, and if we keep winning, my bat mitzvah will be on the same day as a play-off game."

"Oh, no!" I cried before I even had a chance to stop myself.

Zoe's face fell. "There is no way I could have known the Kicks would even have a shot at play-offs when we set the date," she mumbled.

"Of course," Jessi said. "None of us did. But doesn't your ceremony start at four? Our games are almost always in the mornings. Even if we have a play-off game, we should all be able to make it, no problem."

Zoe looked sad. "Yeah, but then I'll be in a big rush to get home from the game to get ready. It sounds really stressful to me. I've been looking forward to my bat mitzvah for years. I want to be able to focus on it completely, not have to worry about play-offs, too."

"Come on." Emma nudged her with her elbow. "We're Super Girls! We can do it all! We can have it all!"

Zoe giggled. "I guess."

"And we'll have fun tomorrow dress shopping." Emma was basically the cheerleader of our group. She always knew how to make people feel better.

Uh-oh. Something just occurred to me. If Emma was the cheerleader of our group, what did that make me? Because I was about to burst Zoe's bubble.

"But there is a problem," I said slowly. "We've got

practice tomorrow. The practice schedule changed so we could get an extra one in before our play-off game against the Tigers this Saturday. Remember?"

Zoe's face fell.

"Can't we just go after practice is over?" Emma asked.

Zoe wrinkled her nose. "No way am I trying on dresses all sweaty and gross from practice."

Jessi shrugged. "It doesn't bother me."

"Or me," Frida added.

"We'll do whatever we can to make this work, Zoe," Emma said, trying to be helpful.

"Then let's all skip practice," Zoe suggested. "We can go straight to Debi's Discount Dresses after school."

Jessi, Emma, and Frida looked as worried as I felt. With our first play-off game coming up in a few days, we needed all the practice we could get.

"Um, Zoe," I began. "If practice gets canceled today because of the rain, and if we miss tomorrow's practice, that gives us only Friday. We need to get as much practice time in as we can before our game on Saturday. It's really important."

"I don't think you understand how important my bat mitzvah is to me," Zoe shot back. Usually Zoe was pretty mellow, but right now she looked upset.

"I'm sorry, Zoe, but there is no way I'm missing practice," I said firmly. "I'll go afterward."

"We *all* will," Emma said.

"Fine," Zoe said. "But I won't be at practice. I'll meet you at Debi's."

Zoe looked more hurt than angry. She stuffed her binder into her book bag before standing up and walking away.

We looked at one another in dismay. I groaned. First the newspaper article, and now this. What a horrible way to start the play-off season!

CHAPTER THREE

Thankfully, Wednesday wasn't all bad. It started to get better during my seventh-period World Civ class. And it definitely wasn't because I had to do four workbook pages on ancient India. It was because of Steven.

Steven was in my grade and was on the boys' soccer team. He had spiky black hair that made him look really cute, and he was nice besides. We would hang out sometimes, and we had two classes together: World Civ and English.

Unfortunately, we sat on total opposite sides of the room in World Civ. He was in the back and I was in the front, so I didn't even get to stare at his hair when I got bored. But lately he'd come up to me after class, and we'd walk to eighth-period English together.

That was what he did on Wednesday. He walked up to me and smiled. Did I mention he had an awesome smile?

"Hey," he said. "I saw that picture of you guys in the paper."

Oh, no, I thought. *The article again!*

"Yeah," I said as we started walking down the hallway. "It was a nice article except for the part where they misquoted me."

He looked sheepish. "I didn't actually read the article."

"Good," I said. "I mean, it's fine and everything, except the reporter wrote . . ."

I hesitated. Did I even want Steven to know the story? But then I realized it was easy to talk to him. He put out this super-sympathetic vibe.

"She wrote that I said that the team wouldn't be anywhere without me, which is totally *not* what I said," I blurted out. "And now some people think I was, like, bragging or whatever."

Steven shrugged. "So what? You're really good."

He reminded me of Maisie, and I smiled. "Thanks. But I still wish the whole thing had never happened."

"You've got a play-off game Saturday, don't you?" he asked, and I nodded. "Well, so do we. I'm sure that's all anybody really cares about, right?"

"Right," I agreed, and then the bell rang. We walked into the classroom. Steven smiled at me again and took his seat next to his friend Cody, who was also on the soccer team. I felt like I was floating on a little cloud as I sat in the desk next to Jessi's.

She looked at me when I sat down.

"I know that smile," she whispered so Steven and Cody wouldn't hear her. "That's a Steven smile."

"Is not!" I lied, but Jessi just shook her head.

It was still raining when the last bell rang, and practice was definitely canceled. When I got home, I decided to get my homework done early, so I went up to my room and turned on my laptop. I was in the middle of my math homework when my inbox popped up on my screen. There was an e-mail from Cassidy Vale.

Hi, Devin,

I understand that your friends might be upset with the quote you gave me. I checked my notes, and verified that you did indeed say what I printed. So I'm afraid I can't run a correction for you.

Sincerely,
Cassidy Vale

"What?" I shrieked.

I stomped downstairs, carrying my laptop. Dad was home from work early, and I found him in the kitchen kneading some pizza dough.

"Dad, you know how I e-mailed that reporter?" I asked. We had all discussed it at dinner the night before.

"Yeah. Did you get a response?" he asked.

"Look at this," I said, thrusting the screen in front of his face. Dad read it, frowning.

"She doesn't seem very professional to me," he said. "I could try calling her during the day tomorrow if you want. Or maybe I'll speak to the editor in chief."

"Forget it." I sighed, thinking of what Steven had said. "I don't want to make a big deal about it. We've got a play-off game to worry about."

Dad nodded thoughtfully. "Let me know if you change your mind, though, okay?"

I smiled gratefully. "Thanks."

Dad nodded to a bowl of broccoli on the counter. "Feel like chopping?"

"In a little bit," I said, glancing at the clock. "I've got to chat with Kara."

"The broccoli will be waiting," Dad said, and I headed back upstairs.

I set up the laptop on my desk and connected to Kara on my webcam. She was my best friend from Connecticut, where I used to live before we moved to California. We video chatted with each other almost every day.

"How did the play thing go?" I asked her.

"It was pretty good," Kara replied. "Sorry I missed you yesterday. We spent, like, two hours in the art room painting the scenery for the play, and when I got home I had a ton of homework. Mom wouldn't let me go online."

"It's okay," I said.

"So, how's *Steven*?" Kara asked, wiggling her eyebrows.

I rolled my eyes. Kara loved to tease me. "He's fine. I told you we met up at the carnival, right?"

Kara nodded. "And you went on the Ferris wheel together. Too bad you didn't get stuck at the top."

I laughed. "You watch too many TV movies!"

"Stuck on top of a Ferris wheel . . . with no choice but to fall in love," Kara said in a dramatic voice.

"You definitely need to meet my friend Frida the next time you come here," I said. "You would love her."

Kara made a silly sad face. "I wish you could come visit here! You could come see the Cosmos in the play-offs."

"It would be hard to just sit in the stands and not jump in and play with you guys," I said. "Anyway, we have *our* first play-off game on Saturday."

"Yay!" Kara cheered. "The Cosmos and the Kicks in the play-offs at the same time. That is so cool."

I smiled. "It's almost like we're in the play-offs together."

"Almost," Kara said. "I have a good feeling. We're both going to win!"

"I hope so," I replied.

"I *know* so," Kara said, and I realized for the millionth time how lucky I was to have her as a friend.

I didn't even tell Kara about the newspaper article thing. I was tired of talking about it. It was time to focus on Saturday's game.

CHAPTER FOUR

I was kind of nervous about practice the next day. Would Grace and the other eighth graders still be mad at me? I hoped that they had forgotten about it.

At first everything seemed to be normal. We all got changed in the locker room in a big hurry after school. Grace and her friends were talking and laughing with one another like they always did, and I did the same with my friends.

Then we all headed over to our practice field. The boys got to use the school field, and we had to cross the street to the community field. Instead of grass it was mostly dirt and weeds, and today it was really muddy from the rain the day before.

"Oh, boy. This is going to get messy," I said as my cleats squished in the mud.

Emma stopped suddenly. "Oh my gosh. Nets!"

I couldn't believe it. For weeks we had been practicing without any nets at the goals. We'd just had some dented garbage cans where either side of the goal would be.

We ran up to Coach Flores, who had a big smile on her face.

"Coach! Where did these come from?" Jessi asked.

"Isn't this great?" she said. "They were donated by Sally Lane, who owns the sporting goods shop in town. She read the article in the paper and wanted to do something to help the team."

"Oh my gosh! They're amazing!" Emma clapped her hands together. "I can't wait to tell Zoe!"

All the girls started talking excitedly about the nets. I was pretty psyched. They would definitely make our practices better, and that was a good thing, especially since we were in the play-offs.

"I have a thank-you card for Ms. Lane," Coach Flores said. "I'd like everyone to sign it, and then we'll warm up."

We all gathered around to sign the card—it was one of those really big ones that are bigger than my head— and then Coach led us in warm-ups. We were all pretty pumped up about the nets, and we ran out onto the field as Coach set up our first drill.

"I want us to work on finishing skills today," she said. Then she counted us off into two groups and had us line up in front of the goal, right outside the penalty box.

She placed three balls between the two lines of players. "Grace, get in the middle," she instructed, and Grace jogged over to the balls. Then Coach pointed to the line of girls on the left of the goal, which I was part of.

"You guys are the attackers," she said, and then she pointed to the right. "And you are the defenders. Grace, I want you to kick a ball to one of the attackers. When Grace kicks the ball to you, attackers, you need to take it to the goal. Defenders, one of you needs to stop the attacker. I'll take goal. Got it?"

We nodded, and Coach ran over to the goal. Then she blew her whistle.

Grace kicked the ball to Giselle, one of her eighth-grade friends. Giselle took off for the goal, and Brianna darted out from the defensive line and tried to get the ball from her, but Giselle got off a shot before Brianna could stop her.

Coach caught the shot with both hands, and then tossed it back to Grace. "Good! Keep going, Grace!"

We got the hang of the drill pretty quickly. Grace kept kicking balls to the girls on the attackers line, and each attacker tried to make it to the goal while the defender tried to block her. I noticed, though, that Grace was kicking the ball to every attacker except me. When she finally did, the ball sailed over my head.

"Sorry, Devin," she said in a flat voice, and I could tell she didn't mean it. I knew she was still mad.

"All right, lines. Switch sides. Devin, you take the middle this time!" Coach called out.

I switched places with Grace. As soon as the lines were

set up, I made a point to shoot the first ball to Grace—properly. I wanted to show her I wasn't going to get into some kind of silly fight with her. If Grace noticed, she didn't show it.

After the drill we had a scrimmage. Even though it was nice to have goals with nets, the field was a total mess, and we kicked up mud and dirt as we ran. By the time practice ended, our legs and uniforms were caked with it.

"We can't go to Debi's Dresses looking like this!" Frida wailed as we walked off the field.

"It's just a little dirt," Emma said.

"Are you serious? We're mud monsters," Frida said.

"Maybe we can shower and change before we go," Jessi suggested.

I pointed to the parking lot, where Jessi's mom's minivan had just pulled up. "It's four-thirty. Zoe's there already. She'll kill us if we're really late."

Emma nodded. "That's true. We'd better go."

We grabbed our bags and jogged up to Mrs. Dukes's car. She popped the hatch for us so we could stow everything in the back. Then we piled in.

"My goodness, you girls are a mess!" she exclaimed.

"The field was supermuddy," Jessi reported, sliding into the front passenger seat. "But we're kind of late as it is. We should get to Debi's."

Mrs. Dukes nodded. "It's not that far."

Debi's Discount Dresses was in a strip mall in Kentville, sandwiched between an Italian restaurant and a store that sold video games. Mrs. Dukes dropped us off in front and went to look for a parking spot, and Emma, Jessi, Frida, and I went inside.

The shop was small with a big 360-degree mirror in the middle and a couple of old-looking couches pushed against the wall. There were racks and racks jammed full of all different kinds of dresses.

Zoe had her back to us because she was looking in a mirror. She had on a hot-pink strapless dress with a short but kind of puffy skirt.

"Oh my gosh! You look gorgeous!" Emma cried.

Zoe spun around. "You're finally here! I just—" She stopped, and her face fell. "You guys are so dirty!"

"We came right from practice," Jessi said quickly. "So come on, let's try on some dresses."

Just then Zoe's mom came out of the back room with another woman, who had short black hair with bangs. She had on a navy-blue dress, black heels, and a silver neck-lace. She looked like one of those people who was always perfectly neat from head to toe.

Zoe's mom looked surprised. "Girls! I didn't realize you had practice today."

"Well, with the play-offs and all . . . ," I said. "We got here as soon as we could."

"Hello, I'm Debi," the dark-haired woman said, pro-nouncing it "de-BEE." She actually tossed her head as she said the "BEE" part, and really elongated the vowels, mak-ing it sound like a fancy European name or something. I felt Emma shake next to me. I looked at her. She grinned as she tried to hold back a laugh.

Debi stared at us in horror for a second before plastering a smile on her face that didn't look exactly real.

"How nice of you to come for your friend," she said, but the way she said it as she took in our mud-splattered clothes made us know she thought it was anything but nice. "However, perhaps we should arrange for another time for you to try on your dresses."

Zoe frowned. "But everyone's here!"

"Zoe, we can always come back," her mother said.

"Can't they just watch and I'll show them the dresses I picked out?" Zoe asked.

Debi nervously eyed her couches. "I'm not sure if that's such a good idea."

Jessi looked at me and rolled her eyes. Those couches had clearly seen better days. I'm not sure what Debi was so worried about, but if she didn't want us in her discount dress shop, what could we do?

"We can come back soon, Zoe, I promise," I said.

Zoe looked like she was going to cry, and then Jessi's eyes lit up.

"Everybody, wait! I've got an idea," she said, and then she ran out of the store.

Emma, Frida, and I looked at each other, too afraid to move and not sure what to do. Finally Emma shrugged and pulled a bag of bright orange cheese puffs out of her backpack and ripped open the top.

Frida frantically shook her head and put her hand to her throat, making a cutting motion. "Don't!" she whispered loudly.

"But I'm always starving after practice," Emma whispered back. She took a cheese puff out of the bag and popped it into her mouth, as a horrified gasp filled the room.

"There is no food in my store!" Debi said, clutching her hand over her heart as her eyes widened in shock. "If you can even call that food!"

"Sorry," Emma mumbled, spraying little orange crumbs out of her mouth. She swallowed and then looked at her hand. The cheese puff had turned her fingers bright orange. She wiped them on her shirt, adding a smear of orange to all the mud.

"Oops," she said as she looked down at her jersey. Debi folded her arms and gave Emma a look like no other. Although, come to think of it, it did remind me of my dad's face when Maisie had dropped his cell phone into the toilet.

Emma smiled sheepishly and put the bag of cheese puffs back into her bag. I glanced at Zoe. She was too miserable to say anything.

Then Jessi ran back in, carrying a bunch of green rain ponchos.

"Mom always has these in the car for soccer games," she said. She pulled one on, the hood making a green point over her head. "See? Instant protection."

Emma giggled. "You look like a gnome."

"I was thinking more like a pea," I said. I took one of the ponchos from Jessi and put it on. "What do you think?" I did a twirl.

"Very fashionable!" Jessi said. "Maybe we can just wear these to the bat mitzvah."

Zoe winced at that as Emma and Frida put their ponchos on too. "You're, like, a supergenius, Jessi," I said. "All the dirt and mud is sealed inside. Debi, your store should be safe."

Zoe looked hopefully at her mom and Debi. The store owner didn't look thrilled, but she reluctantly gave in.

"Please, my name is pronounced 'de-BEE,'" Debi said snootily. She sighed. "Oh, very well. I suppose if you just sit very still and don't go near my dresses," she said. "And, you!" She pointed at Emma. "No more of those orange things!"

Zoe immediately got happy, as if the mud and the cheese puffs had never happened. "Oh, thank you!" Then she turned to us. "I'm trying to decide between this and another dress. And I picked out some that I think would look great on all of you. We can always come back so you can try them on."

"I love the dress you're wearing," Frida said.

Zoe grinned. "Thanks. I kind of love it too. But then there's this other one that's just a little more fashion forward."

We tried not to move around as we waited for Zoe to

return from the dressing room with her mom. Debi went to help some other people who came into the shop, but she kept looking at us to make sure we weren't moving.

Emma glanced at some of the mannequins in the window.

"These dresses are fancy," she remarked. "Do you think I'll have to wear heels?"

I giggled. "Oh my gosh, Emma. You know I love you, but you have a hard time not tripping in sneakers. How could you wear heels?"

"I know!" Emma wailed. "Besides, I'd be, like, eight feet tall!"

We were all giggling now, but we stopped when Zoe came back.

"Wow, that's really cool," I said. This dress was strapless too, with a full skirt, but it was black, and then it had all these silvery flowers sewn down the bodice and on the skirt.

Zoe twirled around in the mirror. "I really like it," she said.

"It's pretty," Emma said. "But the pink one seems more fun."

"And it's a little more youthful," her mother added.

Zoe frowned. "I can't decide!"

"Why don't you show us the dresses you picked out for us?" I suggested. "Maybe you just need to step back, you know?"

Zoe nodded. "Good idea."

So then Zoe gave us a fashion show as she tried on the dresses she thought each of us would like. I guess I should admit that I wasn't superbig on fashion. I didn't wear jeans and T-shirts all the time, like Emma, but I didn't read magazines and watch all the fashion TV shows like Zoe did either. So I was kind of glad that Zoe had some dress ideas.

"Okay, this one's for Frida," Zoe said when she came back wearing a black sleeveless dress with layers of fringe all down the front. It kind of looked like something from the 1920s.

Frida gasped. "That is fabulous!"

"It fits your dark and quirky personality," Zoe remarked. "Plus, I think black looks nice with your hair."

Frida ran a hand through her wavy auburn hair. "Yes, I know," she said in a fake snooty voice. It reminded us all of Debi, and we broke out in giggles. Frida held up her phone. "Let me take a picture."

Zoe posed like a model, and Frida took the shot. Next Zoe put on a dress for Jessi. This one was strapless and straight and made of sparkly silver fabric.

"That's right! I need some bling!" Jessi cried happily, high-fiving me.

"Zoe, you are great at this," I said. I was starting to get excited to see what she had picked out for me. "You could so be a professional stylist."

"Yes, I know," she said, mimicking Frida. "Okay, let me try on Emma's dress."

The next dress she modeled was a shimmering emerald green with a halter-type top, a belt around the waist, and a longer skirt.

"It's the hot color this year," she explained. "And it doesn't look exactly right on me because I'm so short. But it will look perfect on you, Emma."

Emma's eyes were wide; she looked excited and nervous at the same time. "Whatever you say!"

"Me next! Me next!" I was practically bouncing in my seat the way Maisie did when she was excited.

"Okay! Okay!" Zoe said, laughing. She left, and it seemed like forever before she came back, but when she did—I couldn't believe my eyes.

I swear it was the prettiest dress I had ever seen. It was light blue and sleeveless, and the bodice had these silver flowers sewn on one side. The skirt was layers of light ruffles that made me think of clouds and the sky.

"Kicks blue," Zoe said with a grin.

"I love it!" I cried. "What do they call that fabric on the skirt part?"

"It's organza," Zoe answered. "Sometimes organza layers can look like a ballet costume or something, but these are draped in a really natural way. It's going to look great on you."

"Now *I* need to take a picture," I said, and Zoe posed while I snapped one on my phone. I couldn't wait to show Kara.

"I will put these dresses aside until you girls can come

back for a fitting and your parents can buy the dresses for you," Debi said, walking up with a clipboard in her hand. "Just give me your sizes."

When Debi was done with us, we carefully stood up and packed up the ponchos. Zoe had changed back into her regular clothes.

"Sorry about being so dirty," I said. "The field was really muddy today."

"I'm glad you guys came," Zoe said. "And I'm sorry I missed practice. But this is a big deal for me, you know? I've been waiting for this for, like, my whole life."

I nodded. It was kind of how I felt about getting into the play-offs.

"When we come back, we'll be clean," Jessi promised.

"I certainly hope so," Debi said loudly, and Jessi and I looked at each other, trying not to crack up.

We tumbled outside, laughing.

"I thought she was going to clean us off with a fire hose," Jessi said.

"Actually, that sounds like fun right now," Emma said.

I sniffed the air. "You know, I just realized that we probably smell as bad as we look."

Frida shuddered. "Let's just get home and shower, please."

Jessi's mom pulled up, and we all piled into the minivan. Picking out dresses had been pretty easy. I just hoped that beating the Tigers would be easy too!

CHAPTER FIVE

I could swear a bunch of butterflies were doing a little dance in my stomach as Dad pulled into the Newton Middle School parking lot Saturday morning. It was an hour before game time, but Dad, Mom, and Maisie had come to get good seats for the game while I warmed up with the team.

The last time we'd played the Tigers, they had destroyed us, but that was before we'd gotten our act together as a team. I knew the Tigers would be confident going in, and it looked like their fans were too. They had tied about a hundred black and orange balloons to the fence surrounding the field, and the stands were already filled with Tigers fans wearing black and orange.

As we walked toward the field, I looked back at my family and was grateful that they were all wearing Kicks blue.

"So when you win this game, do you get a big trophy or something?" Maisie asked.

I shook my head. "No, but close. This is just the first round of the play-offs. If we win today, we'll have to go on and play one more team. If we beat them, we'll get the division trophy. We'll be league champions!"

"And then they can go on to enter the early rounds of the state championships," Dad said, and I felt a little shiver of excitement.

The state championships! There was actually a chance that we could win state, just like the Kicks had when Coach Flores had played on the team. I felt the butterflies flutter again, and then I told myself to focus. We had to win this game first.

I felt a little more comfortable when we got a view of the away-team stands and I saw some blue shirts. There were a lot of Kicks on the field already.

"See you later!" I said, and then I ran toward my team.

"Good luck, honey!" Mom called out. "And don't forget—"

"To hydrate! I know!" I called over my shoulder. I think Mom thought I was going to shrivel up and turn to dust out on the field.

I caught up with the rest of the team and tossed my duffel bag onto the sidelines. Everyone was stretching or talking or walking—you could almost see the nervous energy in the air.

Anna was jumping up and down.

"Anna, what are you doing?" I asked.

"Can't . . . stop . . . jumping," she said, her curly hair bouncing on top of her head.

I shook my head and walked over to Jessi.

"Everybody's, like, freaking out," she said.

"No kidding," I replied. "I hope we can keep it together on the field."

Frida ran up to us. "Devin, any ideas for me today? I can't think of anything."

Frida always played better when she pretended she was someone else on the field. It might sound weird, but it totally worked for her.

"How about a *Wizard of* Oz thing?" I suggested. "You're Dorothy, and the other team's players are flying monkeys, trying to capture you."

Frida nodded. "That could work. And you guys could all be my friends, the munchkins."

"Hey! I'm no munchkin," Jessi protested.

"I'll be a munchkin," piped up Zoe, who had been behind us the whole time. "I'm the right height, anyway."

"Can I be a witch?" Emma asked, overhearing us.

"No, you need to be that guy who guards the Emerald City gates, because you're the goalie," Frida said.

Emma wrinkled her nose. "Didn't he have a mustache?"

"You might look cute with a mustache," Zoe said. She put a lock of Emma's long black hair under Emma's nose. "See? Not bad?"

"So it's settled. I'm Dorothy," Frida said. She looked

down at her cleats. "Too bad I can't wear ruby slippers out there."

We were all cracking up when Grace's voice cut through everyone's talking.

"Sock swap, everybody!" she yelled.

As we got into a circle to do our sock swap, I couldn't help thinking that Grace had been acting kind of different lately. She was always pretty quiet, and almost never called for the sock swap.

It's ever since the article came out, I thought, but I pushed the thought away. The last thing I wanted to think about today was that stupid article.

Emma nudged me out of my thoughts and handed me a pink sock with green polka dots.

"Oh, thanks," I said. Then I quickly took off my right sock—Kicks blue with white stripes—and handed it to Jessi on my left. Then I put on Emma's sock. We had been doing the sock swap since our first game, and it had become a Kicks tradition.

When we had our cleats back on, Coach Flores got us into a huddle.

"We've still got some time before the game, so I think we should warm up with some simple drills," she said. "You guys have been working really well as a team lately. Just keep that up and you're going to do great."

I glanced at Grace. I hoped we were still working as a team. We all piled hands on top of one another in the middle of the circle and let out a cheer.

"Gooooooo, Kicks!"

We dribbled and practiced passing for a little while, and then the refs started coming out onto the field. Coach called us into a huddle again.

"Emma, I want you to start on goal," she said. "Giselle, Anjali, Frida, you're on defense. Midfield is Jessi, Grace, Maya, and Taylor. Devin, Zoe, and Megan, I want you on the forward line. Got it?"

We nodded. Coach was basically putting up our strongest players first, in the positions we all played best. Not a bad strategy to start off an important game.

Then Grace went out for the coin toss, which we won, and we chose to receive the ball first. I took a deep breath as I ran out onto the field to take my place.

Then the ref's whistle blew, and the Tigers player kicked the ball pretty deep into our midfield. Jessi stopped it with her foot and then dribbled it down the right side as two Tigers charged for her. One of them stole it right out from under her and passed it to another Tigers striker farther down the field. That Tiger started dribbling it toward the goal, but Frida zipped in front of her.

"Follow the Yellow Brick Road!" she yelled, kicking the ball away from the striker. It was a wild kick that went out of bounds, but it was worth it to see the look on the striker's face. Frida grinned at me as I jogged past her.

"It was a ruby slipper malfunction," Frida said sheepishly.

The Tigers player tossed the ball in from the sidelines, and the play continued up and down the field. The soccer ball bounced from player to player like a ball bouncing off bumpers in a pinball machine. Every time we got control of it, one of the Tigers got it away from us—and we did the same to their attackers. I think the Tigers were a little surprised to see us putting up such a good fight.

Then one of the Tigers found herself surrounded by Kicks, so she kicked the ball hard across the field to one of her teammates. Grace was all over it, intercepting it and making a mad dash to the goal straight down the middle of the field. None of the Tigers could catch up to her.

"Go, go, go, go, go, go, go!" I yelled, and I could hear the other Kicks yelling behind me. The Tigers goalie had her hands on her knees, ready to dive, jump, or catch, trying to anticipate what Grace would do.

Grace waited until she was about twenty feet away from the goal, when she kicked it hard and fast—not too high and not too low. For a second I thought the goalie might catch it, but it flew just over her head. She jumped, reaching for it, and it brushed her fingertips as it went into the goal.

"Whoooo!" I hollered and high-fived Zoe, the closest player to me. The rest of the girls erupted into cheers and hugs. But there wasn't much time to celebrate, because the Tigers set up for kickoff just seconds after the goal.

"There's no place like home! There's no place like home!" Frida yelled down the field.

"Nice one!" I said to Grace as she caught up with us, but she didn't say anything in response.

The Kicks and the Tigers did the back-and-forth pin-ball thing for a while, and then suddenly the Tigers were all over the Kicks goal, passing the ball back and forth to each other so that our defenders were practically running in circles trying to stop them.

"Curse you, flying monkeys!" Frida cried.

Emma got confused too, running back and forth across the goal, trying to keep pace with the ball. Then a Tiger made another quick, short pass to a teammate, who headed it right into a wide-open part of the net. Emma wasn't anywhere near it.

There wasn't much time left after that, and the first half ended in a tie, 1–1.

We jogged back to the bench. I grabbed my water bottle and held it up to the stands so my mom could see me take a big, long drink.

"You guys are doing great out there," Coach said. "Defense, they tuckered you out in those last ten minutes, so I want to put in Jade, Olivia, and Alandra when the half starts. Zarine, you go in for Emma for a while. Brianna, you go in for Megan, and Anna, you go in for Maya."

I saw Megan frown, and I knew she didn't like being taken out of the game. But I understood Coach. She took me out sometimes too.

When the second half started, the Tigers had control of the ball. I got lucky when one of the Tigers passed the ball right in front of me, and I stopped it with my foot. The two players converged on me, so I passed the ball to Zoe.

"Zoe, do your lightning thing!" I yelled. Zoe's size and speed meant that she could zigzag her way through defenders so fast, they didn't know where to turn. She got all the way down to the goal and made a solid shot, but this time the Tigers goalie stopped it.

The Tigers took the ball all the way down to our goal, and one of their strikers sent a shot skidding toward Zarine. She made a spectacular dive, stopping it with her body.

"Way to go, Zarine!" Emma yelled from the sidelines.

The second half sped by. We went back and forth up and down the field. Coach put Emma back in when Zarine got tired, and she switched up some of the midfielders, too, when she had a chance. A few minutes before the game ended, we were still tied 1–1, and she sent Megan back in to sub for Zoe.

That's when we finally got a break. One of the Tigers kicked the ball out of bounds, and Taylor tossed it in.

Jessi got it and headed it right to me. We were pretty close to the Tigers goal, and I had a clear path right to it.

"Devin! Over here! Over here!"

Megan was running parallel to me. I know she wanted me to pass it to her, but there were two Tigers defenders about to overtake her, and I didn't want to risk it.

So I did the next best thing. I faked like I was going to pass to Megan, and while the goalie's head was turned, I kicked the ball right into the goal.

"Go, Devin!" I heard Jessi and Brianna cheer, and I felt like I was floating.

Then, to my amazement, the ref's whistle blew. Game over!

Jessi ran up to me and hugged me so hard, I couldn't breathe.

"Devin, you did it! We won the game!"

"We're heading to the league championships!" I heard Coach Flores shout over the Kicks' excited voices. "Who would have thought we would get to the championships back at the start of the season? We've come so far, and I'm so proud of all of you."

I felt like those butterflies inside me were making me float off the ground. We'd won! And my goal had broken the tie! Now we had a shot at being the league champions!

And then I heard Megan behind me.

"Oh, good," she said in a flat, sarcastic voice. "Devin saves the day again."

The butterflies floated away, taking my happiness with them. Jessi must have seen my face.

"Don't let it get to you, Devin," she said. "We won!"

"I know," I said, but I didn't feel like a winner. What was the point of winning when half of my teammates hated me?

CHAPTER SIX

"Come on, Devin." Emma draped an arm around my shoulder, trying to cheer me up. "Let's go celebrate with some ice cream!"

"Wait! What time is it?" I asked.

"It's one-thirty, and by the way, congratulations!" I heard my dad's voice behind me, and I whirled around. He grabbed me into a big hug. "Way to go, Devin! You did great."

My mom and Maisie were with him. "Congrats, sweetie! I know how hard you worked for this." My mom smiled at me as she gave me a hug too.

"That was really cool," Maisie said, smiling. Yeah, she could be pretty cute and nice when she wanted to. She ran around on the soccer field, mimicking my last goal of the game. "Boom!" She pretended to kick the ball toward the goal. "And the crowd goes wild!" Maisie held her hands up in the air triumphantly as we all laughed.

"So, I think I heard something about ice cream to celebrate?" my dad asked.

"Actually, I was hoping we could cheer on our fellow Kangaroos," I explained. "The boys' first play-off game is today at two. It's an away game at Riverdale. Can you give us a ride?"

My dad nodded. "Sure thing!"

"Let me ask my parents!" Emma said before racing off. I went to find Jessi, Frida, and Zoe.

They were standing together, but something seemed wrong. Frida's face was flushed bright red, and Jessi had her arms crossed tightly in front of her. Zoe had a frown on her face.

"What's wrong?" I asked.

Jessi shook her head. "Nothing, it's nothing."

I glanced up and saw Megan and Giselle walking away.

"Um, okay," I said, not believing her, but since my dad was waiting, I didn't get into it. "So, do you guys want to go cheer on the boys at their Rams game?"

Jessi's eyes widened. "Of course! I told Cody I would try to come."

Frida grinned. "I bet you did. Who wouldn't want to see Captain Kiss in action?"

Jessi shrieked. "Frida!" But Frida had already raced behind me to hide. She had made up that silly nickname once when she had been teasing Jessi about her crush on Cody. Whenever Frida said "Captain Kiss," Jessi would pretend to be super-angry at her and chase her around.

"We don't have time for this! The game starts in a little bit, and my dad is going to give us a ride, but there is really no time to change," I told them.

Jessi stopped in the middle of lunging toward Frida. "No problem. We're already wearing Kentville blue to show our support!" she said, gesturing to her uniform.

But Zoe frowned. "I was going to work on party plans this afternoon. . . ."

"You'll have plenty of time after the game to plan away," Frida poked her head out from behind my back to say to her. "Come with us, Zoe, please?"

Zoe's face softened. "Oh, okay. I guess I have time."

After my dad arranged everything with all of the parents, we piled into the minivan and got to the field. We were late. The game had already started.

Zoe, Emma, and I were walking toward the bleachers, with Frida and Jessi right behind us. I heard them angrily whispering to each other.

"We should tell her!" Frida whispered loudly.

"It will only make Devin upset!" Jessi was so insistent that she forgot to whisper, and I easily heard her.

I turned around. "What will make me upset?"

Jessi turned to Frida. "Great, look what you've done!"

"What I've done? You're the one with the big mouth!" Frida shot back.

I remembered how flustered they had looked when I'd seen them after the game was over. "Does this have anything to do with Megan and Giselle? You all looked angry when I came over. Right when Megan and Giselle were walking away."

Zoe and Emma had stopped and were listening to the conversation.

"Just tell her," Zoe said softly.

Frida sighed. "Look, Megan was really mad after the game. She said she was wide open, but instead of passing to her you took the shot, and it was only luck that it was a goal."

Jessi shook her head. "It gets worse. Giselle called you a ball hog."

"What? That's crazy!" I felt my cheeks turn red with anger. "There were two Tigers defenders on Megan. If I had passed to her, the ball would have been intercepted. I know it! I knew my best bet was taking the shot. And it worked!"

"That's what I told her," Jessi said angrily.

"And me too!" Frida chimed in, at the same time as Zoe.

"They wouldn't listen to us," Zoe added sadly. "And there's more. Megan said all the eighth graders agreed that you were hogging the ball and were trying to be the star of the game."

"And they said we shouldn't pass the ball to you anymore so you would learn a lesson," Frida said. "As if!"

"Did they really ask you to do that?" I asked, shocked.

Jessi nodded. "They want the entire team to not pass to you. But I told them no way!"

Ugh! I smacked my forehead with my palm. "This thing with the eighth graders is getting worse. It's definitely not blowing over!" I groaned.

Emma wrinkled her forehead as she frowned. "Maybe we should tell Coach."

"No!" I cried. "It will just make things worse."

Just then the cheering of the crowd distracted us.

"Let's forget about it for now," I said, "and watch the game."

"I'm starving," Emma said. "Let's sit near the snack stand."

We quickly found seats in the away section, right next to the snack stand. Emma got some fries, and Frida ordered the cheese nachos, but I wasn't hungry. I slumped over as I sat down and put my chin in my hands, my elbows resting on my knees.

Emma and Jessi immediately began stomping their feet on the metal bleachers. "The Rams are the ones that we're gonna defeat! So come on, everybody, get the Kangaroo beat!" they yelled in unison.

"Um, guys," Zoe said, her eyes round as she pointed to a bunch of kids standing at the snack stand. They were all wearing red and yellow, Riverdale colors, and were giving us annoyed looks.

Emma and Jessi just looked at each other and burst out laughing. "We are on Riverdale's field. What did we expect?" Emma asked between giggles.

"Is that Jamie?" I poked Jessi in the ribs before pointing to a girl with long blond hair. She was wearing a Riverdale jersey and scowling at us.

"It sure is." Jessi's eyes narrowed. "I guess she's still mad about us beating out the Rams for a spot in the play-offs. Tough!" Jessi raised her voice loud enough for Jamie to hear her. "Get over it!"

Jamie turned toward us. "Let's go," she said to her teammates as she wrinkled her nose slightly. "Something suddenly stinks around here."

"Yeah, and it's you!" Jessi said. Then she stuck her tongue out at Jamie. Emma started laughing hysterically again, but Zoe tapped Jessi on the arm. "Hey! Don't stoop to their level."

"You're right. We are heading to the league championship. No need to hold a grudge," Jessi said with a shrug. But the damage was done.

"Come on," Jamie said tersely to her friends before they stomped angrily away.

"What a sore loser," I said. "And after everything she did to us! We're the ones who should be mad at her."

Jamie had pulled a lot of mean pranks to make sure the Rams would beat the Kicks in the last game before play-offs. But it hadn't worked. In the end the Kicks had faced the Rams on the field and beat them fair and square.

"Whatever." Jessi rolled her eyes. "It's about the boys' team today. How's Cody doing?" she asked as she sat forward, her eyes on the field.

Since it had taken us so long to get settled, we'd ended up missing a lot of the game.

"The score is zero–zero," Frida said. "It looks like this is going to be a close one. No one is giving an inch!"

The Rams offense was putting a ton of pressure on the Kangaroos defense, but the Kangaroos were holding their own. But as the game wore on, our defense began to get tired out. At the game half we could hear Coach Valentine talking to the boys. Loudly.

"Get it together, men!" he barked. He sat out some of the players and put in some new, fresh players.

Then he paced back and forth in front of the benched players, telling them in detail where they'd gone wrong.

"Dylan! I told you to shoot wide, not high! Adam, you know that a player misses all of the shots that he doesn't take. Look for openings!" He kept going on and on.

"I'm so glad he's not our coach," Zoe said with a shudder.

"I feel so bad for them," Frida said. She cupped her hands over her mouth. "Go, Kangaroos!"

We all joined in shouting encouragement, hoping to give the boys a boost. At first it seemed like it might have worked. The Kangaroos definitely had some more pep in their step, but unfortunately so did the Rams. The Kangaroos' attacks seemed stronger now, and one of the Kangaroos got a good shot, but the Rams goalie shot straight into the air to make a spectacular save, catching the ball with the very tips of his fingers.

"What does he have, trampolines in his cleats?" Emma wondered. Even though we were rooting for Kentville, we all couldn't help but be impressed.

I spotted Cody and his teammate Michael using short passes to carry the ball down the field.

"Just watch!" Jessi said, grabbing my arm. "Cody's got this!"

Steven hung back, sneaking up as he tried not to draw the attention of the Rams. Cody spotted him and sent the ball flying his way, just as a Ram swooped in to intercept. The shot went wide. Steven dove for it, and managed to connect. His hard kick went high, sailing toward the goal. But once again the Rams goalie made what looked like an impossible jump and batted the ball back.

The Rams fans cheered, while we groaned. A few minutes later one of the Rams scored, and the crowd went wild. The momentum was firmly on the Rams side now.

I had to hand it to the Kangaroos. They didn't back down, even though the tide had turned. Our defense tightened up, and not another goal got through, but the Kangaroos couldn't make any headway on scoring themselves. The game ended 1–0, Rams. The boys' play-off dreams were over.

"Poor Cody!" Jessi dug her fingers into my arm. "He must be so upset!"

"I'm pretty sure they all are," Frida reminded her. "They're a team, remember?"

I let out a big sigh. I felt bad for all of the Kangaroos, but I knew where Jessi was coming from. I could only imagine how Steven was feeling right now. If we had lost our play-off game to the Tigers, I would have been totally bummed out.

"Let's go say hi," Emma suggested. "Maybe we can cheer them up."

"Good idea!" Jessi jumped to her feet, and we followed the crowd down the stairs and to the field.

Some of the Kangaroos were already heading out with their families, but Steven and Cody were huddled together on the sideline, talking.

"Hey," Jessi said. "Great game. You guys really toughed it out. Sorry it ended the way it did."

"I thought your one kick was a goal for sure," I told Steven. "That was some save the Rams goalie made."

"Yeah," Steven mumbled without even looking at me. "You ready, dude?" he said to Cody. Cody nodded.

"Let's go," Cody said, and together they walked off without saying another word to us.

I looked at Jessi and saw the hurt, confused look in her eyes. I might as well have been looking in the mirror, because I knew the same expression was on my own face. I knew Steven and Cody were just upset about their loss, but their reaction stung anyway.

"Hi, Devin!" Kara's big blue eyes were glowing with happiness when I logged in for our video chat later that afternoon. I didn't even have to ask.

"The Cosmos won!" I cried happily.

Kara nodded. "We sure did! Four to two! How did you guys do?"

"We won too," I told her. But she read my tampered enthusiasm right away.

Kara frowned. "What's up, Devin? You sounded more excited about the Cosmos winning."

I sighed. "Don't get me wrong. I'm so totally excited that we won." I paused, not even sure where to begin. I hadn't told Kara the story about the newspaper article because I'd been so sure it was going to blow over. But now I told her everything.

"They called you a ball hog and told the other girls not to pass to you!" Kara exclaimed. She made this frowny, mad face that she'd been making since preschool. The first time I saw her make it was when the teacher gave her graham crackers instead of animal crackers for a snack. I laughed so hard, milk squirted out of my nose. It just looked that silly. And it has made me laugh ever since. But thankfully I didn't squirt milk out of my nose anymore. That was not a good look for me.

I let out a long belly laugh. It felt good after all the highs and lows of this crazy day.

"Thanks," I said as I finally stopped laughing. "I needed that." Usually when I started laughing over the frowny face, Kara forgot whatever it was she was mad about. But not today.

"Seriously, Devin, those girls are mean!" Kara was still angry. "You need to say something."

"We just won our first play-off game. They have to let this go. Don't they?" I asked hopefully.

Kara blew out a deep breath. "If they don't, you really need to talk to the coach about it. It's one thing if they're mad. It's another if they're bullying you over it or trying to get the other players to not pass you the ball."

"Let me give it some more time," I told her. "Maybe they were just angry after the game and didn't really mean it, about not passing the ball to me. But if not, I guess I'll have to talk to Coach." I sighed. "Why does this have to be so complicated? We just won our first play-off game! We should be celebrating. They've got to stop being mad at me."

"I hope you're right," Kara said.

"I forgot the other bad news." I filled her in on how the boys' team had lost.

"And then Steven totally blew me off after the game," I said as I made my own frowny, mad face.

"Wait! Are you *sure* he didn't say anything else?" Kara asked.

"Positive," I sighed.

"He was just disappointed, that's all," Kara said. "After all, it had just happened. It's not like he even had time to wrap his head around being booted from the play-offs before you showed up."

"I know. You're right," I said. Kara always knew how to make me feel better. "And on the bright side, both the Cosmos and the Kicks are still in the play-offs!"

"State championships, here we come!" Kara grinned.

As a team the Kicks had come so far. At the start of

the season nobody would have thought we could make it to the league championships, let alone even have a shot at state. We were all finally playing to our full potential. Coach was awesome and really motivating us. It would stink if this stupid newspaper article caused a rift in the team that would hurt our playing. If we wanted to be champions, the Kicks had to start getting along!

CHAPTER SEVEN

"So Jessi will marry Jake Washington, and they will live together in an apartment in Rio de Janeiro, where Jessi will work as a graphic designer. They'll drive around in a PT Cruiser and have ten kids!" Frida read from her notebook, and everyone started laughing.

We were sitting outside in the library courtyard at lunch on Monday. Frida was leading us in a game of MASH, which was supposed to predict your future. I loved how silly all the outcomes were.

"I don't know how you'll fit all those kids into a PT Cruiser," Emma said, and laughed.

I wiggled my eyebrows at Jessi. "So, Jake Washington, eh?" He was in our gym class.

"Coming up with the names of four boys wasn't easy. Wait until it's your turn!" Jessi said. Of course, Cody had been the first boy she had named. Frida had then counted and randomly crossed off an item from each list: boys, careers, numbers, cities, types of cars, and MASH (which stood for "mansion, apartment, shack, or house") until only one remained for each.

Frida turned to Zoe. "Your turn! First, name four boys."

Zoe shrugged. "I don't even know if I ever want to get married."

"Fine," Frida said. "We'll skip that part. Name four jobs."

As Frida and Zoe played, Jessi turned to me.

"I heard Coach Flores wasn't here to teach her gym classes today," she said to me. "I wonder if we'll have practice."

"They would have made an announcement in homeroom if it was canceled, right?" I asked. Practices were rarely canceled, but when they were, an announcement was made over the school's PA system.

"Maybe she'll be in later," Brianna said. Today she, Sarah, and Anna were eating lunch with us.

Talking about practice made me think about if the eighth graders really wouldn't pass the ball to me. "I wonder if the eighth graders are still mad at me," I said. "I was on MyBook on Sunday. Usually after a game I'd chat with Grace and we'd go over everything. You know, talk about what worked and what didn't for the team. But I didn't hear from her."

Brianna shifted in her chair, and I saw Anna's brown eyes grow even wider as she shot Brianna a look.

I sighed. "Just tell me. What is it now?"

Brianna tossed her long blond hair over her shoulder. She was very straightforward, so I knew she'd tell me the truth.

"Alandra and Zarine were calling you a ball hog," Brianna said, "when we were all chatting online on Saturday night."

"I told them they were being totally unfair," Anna chimed in. "I saw that play. You would have been stupid to pass the ball to Megan."

Sarah nodded. "I said the same thing. But then they said something really nuts."

I groaned. "Let me guess. They told you not to pass the ball to me, right?"

"Yep," Anna said. "I said they were crazy. How is that any way for a team to play? Especially with the championship coming up."

"When we told them that, Alandra said it would be only for a couple of practices. So you would learn to be more 'humble,'" Brianna said, and rolled her eyes. "She said that was what Grace wanted, and since Grace was the eighth-grade captain, we should listen to her. For the good of the team."

"I couldn't believe what I was hearing," Sarah said. "I told them there was no way that could be good for the team."

"Then Zarine said that since Grace is the eighth-grade captain, she has seniority over Devin and we should listen to her," Anna said. "And when we all said we wouldn't do it, they just stopped talking to us."

I groaned. "Great. The seventh graders versus the eighth graders. Just the kind of team unity we need for our next play-off game," I said sarcastically.

Frida looked up from the MASH game and put a hand over her heart. "A soccer team divided against itself cannot stand," she said solemnly. Then she smiled. "But on the bright side, Zoe is going to be a fashion designer and live in a mansion in Paris!"

Zoe had a huge smile on her face. "I hope that does come true!"

"Can you do a MASH for the Kicks? Because I'm worried about our team's future," I said with a frown.

"Let's see what happens at practice today," Emma suggested. "If they still seem mad, maybe we should try to talk it out."

"I guess," I said. "I'll try anything at this point!"

When I walked into the locker room with Jessi before practice, I felt the butterflies in my stomach doing the cha-cha. How were the eighth graders going to act toward me?

A hush fell over Grace, Taylor, Anjali, and Megan, who'd been talking when we'd first walked in. They looked away and wouldn't make eye contact with me.

I was surprised to feel the butterflies disappear. I wasn't nervous anymore, just angry. This was ridiculous!

"Grace, can I talk to you for a second?" I asked, gesturing to the bathroom.

Grace frowned. "I guess."

We walked into the bathroom together, and I turned to face Grace.

"Look, I get that you are mad at me about the newspaper article. I'm totally telling the truth that I did not say that quote." Grace's face remained stiff. "You can believe me or not. That's up to you. But can't we get along, for the good of the team?"

"You know, I'm not the only one who's mad. A lot of the other girls are too," Grace said, her arms crossed in front of her.

"You mean a lot of the eighth graders," I pointed out. "And you should know that a lot of the seventh graders are mad that you asked the entire team not to pass the ball to me."

"I never said that!" Grace said, her voice rising.

"That's not what I heard," I shot back. "And I think it's really immature."

"So you want me to believe you about the newspaper article, but you won't believe me about this?" Grace fumed.

I hadn't thought of it like that. I stared at Grace, not knowing what to say. After all, I had heard from Brianna the thing about it being Grace who wanted everyone not to pass the ball to me, and Brianna had heard it from someone else on MyBook. There were always lots of rumors on MyBook. Who knew for sure if it was true? But before I could admit that to Grace, she turned and stormed out of the locker room.

Things had just gone from bad to worse!

Once I was back in the locker room, I decided to steer clear of Grace until she had time to cool off. Then I would try to talk to her again. If she didn't want to talk to me, then I'd have to let Coach Flores know what was going on. She'd know what to do.

Jessi looked at me curiously. "What happened?" she whispered.

"I'll tell you later," I said back. I didn't want anyone overhearing us. I changed quickly and headed for the door.

But all of us—both seventh and eighth graders—were in for a shock once we got on the field for practice. Instead of Coach Flores's smiling face, we were greeted with the tall, imposing figure of Coach Valentine, the boys' soccer coach. He blew sharply into his whistle.

"Listen up!" he said loudly. "Coach Flores was called away on a family emergency. I'll be subbing in for her until she gets back."

Olivia, one of my teammates, whispered into my ear. "But isn't he the boys' coach?"

"Yes, but the boys lost on Saturday, so their season is over," I whispered back.

"You!" Coach Valentine yelled, pointing right at me. "Do you have something to say?"

I felt my face turn red. "No, sorry," I mumbled.

"No, sorry, what?" he asked.

"No, sorry, very sorry?" I was totally confused.

"It's 'No, sorry, Coach!'" he said. "You will always address me as 'Coach.' All of you. Understood?"

I looked around at my teammates' faces. The expressions were a mixture of horror and fear. Everyone yelled, "Yes, Coach!"

Anna came running onto the field, panting. "Sorry I'm late," she started, then looked up at Coach Valentine, surprised. "What's going—"

Coach Valentine blew into his whistle. "Drop and give me twenty push-ups, all of you! When you're done, you'll run five laps around the field. If anyone shows up late, the entire team is punished. Got it?"

Yikes! I quickly hit the ground, scared not to do what he said. Once, we had shared a practice with the boys' team. Coach Valentine had seemed tough, but not this tough. Maybe because Coach Flores had been there to balance him out.

Jessi was on my side. She checked to make sure Coach Valentine wasn't looking before quickly whispering to me: "I hope Coach Flores is okay!"

"Yeah, and I hope she gets back soon!" I whispered back as I finished my push-ups. We jumped to our feet and started our laps. Usually when doing laps we would chat and joke around, but today everyone ran in silence, afraid to speak. While we were running, Coach Valentine set up cones around the field.

As we finished our laps, we lined up in front of Coach Valentine.

He blew his whistle again. "We're going to be doing a passing/receiving exercise." He explained.

Grace raised her hand.

"What is it?" he barked at her.

"Today is my day to run some drills," she said. "I have something already planned. It's a drill that will work on receiving, turning, dribbling, and shooting."

I heard a few of the girls gasp at Grace's courage.

"What do you mean it's your day to run the drills?" Coach Valentine asked her.

"Devin and I are the team captains," Grace explained. "Coach Flores lets us each run one practice per week."

"And who is Devin?" Coach Valentine wondered.

I stepped forward. "Me, Coach."

"Listen up, all of you," he said. "That may have been the way Coach Flores ran practice, but it's not the way I do things. When Coach Flores gets back, you can run all the drills you want. But for now I'm in charge of what we do. Understood?"

Grace and I both nodded. I felt like I was in boot camp instead of at soccer practice.

"Yes, Coach!" I said. I had to stop myself from saluting.

Coach quickly organized some of us into the spaces between the cones, and others into the middle of the field. The players in the middle would pass to the players between the cones, with Coach calling out variations along the way. If there had been some plan to not pass me the ball, it didn't happen. No one would try anything out of the ordinary that would put them under the scrutiny of Coach Valentine!

I had to admit, it was a pretty good drill, and it helped a lot with our passing and receiving techniques. But the usual joking around was gone. Everyone looked grim-faced and serious, more like prisoners than middle school soccer players.

"Cheer up, girls. You're not at a funeral!" Coach yelled. "I know I tell my players to kill it on the field, but it's only a figure of speech."

He then started laughing loudly at his own joke. We all looked around at one another with shocked faces. Coach Valentine, laughing?

But then, just as quickly as he'd started laughing, he stopped. "Count off for scrimmage!" he barked after toot-ing his whistle to signify the drill was over.

We quickly counted off ones and twos and divided ourselves on the field. I was on the same team as Grace. Maybe, just maybe, she was too mad at Coach Valentine to still be mad at me. I gave her a small smile to test the waters. But she didn't smile back before quickly looking away. I wasn't surprised. And now there was no Coach Flores to turn to. I certainly wasn't going to tell Coach Valentine about it!

Finally, practice was over. "Nice hustle," Coach Valentine said. "I can see why you girls made the play-offs."

I looked at Jessi, her mouth forming a surprised O. I guessed Coach Valentine could be nice, after all.

"I'll see you all here for practice tomorrow—on time," he added threateningly.

"But, Coach," Frida said, a note of urgency in her voice. "We weren't supposed to have practice on Tuesday. I have my acting class."

"And I have to meet with my party planner!" Zoe moaned.

"Acting classes? Party planners?" Coach Valentine asked in disbelief. "Do the rest of you have plans to go skipping through a field of daisies?" He started laughing loudly at his own joke again. Emma stood next to me, and I could hear her choking back a giggle.

But once again his attitude quickly changed. "Do I need to remind you that you are in the play-offs?" Coach Valentine roared as soon as he stopped laughing. "You should be eating, breathing, and sleeping nothing but soccer! I'll see you all tomorrow. Understood?"

Everyone nodded. Emma nudged me in the ribs with her elbow. "Yes, Coach!" she said, and then everyone else joined in, me included.

The sooner Coach Flores got back, the better!

CHAPTER EIGHT

"Please, please tell me you have good news for me," I pleaded as I draped my bag around the cafeteria chair before sitting down.

Coach Flores still hadn't been back on Tuesday, but I had all of my fingers crossed that she'd be back in time for today's practice.

I looked hopefully at Jessi, Emma, Zoe, and Frida.

Jessi slowly shook her head. "Sorry, Devin, but we've got another practice with Coach Valentine to look forward to today."

"Coach Flores is still out," Emma added sadly.

"Oh, no!" I said. "I don't know if I can take another practice with him."

Frida shuddered. "Yesterday was even worse than Monday. 'Hollywood! Get the lead out!'" Frida did a perfect imitation of Coach Valentine's gruff voice. Ever since he'd heard about Frida's acting classes, he'd started calling her "Hollywood."

"My arms are still sore from all the push-ups," Zoe complained.

I rubbed my own arms. They were a little sore too. When Olivia had showed up late at yesterday's practice, we'd all had to run laps. It had gotten worse when Gabriela had come late too. We'd had to do, like, a zillion push-ups.

"Well, at least we got a great workout," I said jokingly.

"Yeah, at the expense of me missing my acting class," Frida complained.

"And me missing my meeting with my party planner," Zoe said. "We were going to do a cake tasting!"

Jessi raised an eyebrow. "It sounds more like you're planning a wedding than a bat mitzvah!"

"I told you, everything has to be perfect, down to the last detail," Zoe said, totally serious. "You guys don't get it. All of my older sisters had perfect bat mitzvahs. Every single person in my family will be there, including my cousins from New Jersey. If I have to taste every cake in the Kentville area, so be it."

Emma started cracking up. "Let Zoe eat cake!"

"Now, that's the kind of party planning I can do! Do you need some help eating all that cake, Zoe?" Jessi asked.

Zoe laughed. "I know I sound nuts, but I really want this to be a day everyone will remember," she said.

"I wish I could forget practice with Coach Valentine," Frida said dramatically, dropping her head into her hands.

"I'm traumatized. And I'm not sure which is more trau-matic—his corny jokes or his constant yelling. "

Jessi shuddered. "It's like having Dr. Jekyll and Mr. Hyde as a soccer coach!"

I let out a big sigh. Even though Coach Valentine's methods were way different from anything I had ever experienced before, I felt like I was learning some good pointers from his practices. But I needed to talk to Coach Flores about the problems we were having as a team!

Emma heard me sigh and gave me a sympathetic grin. "Have there been any more problems with the eighth graders, Devin?"

I nodded. "Grace still won't talk to me." I had filled them in yesterday at lunch about our conversation in the bathroom. "I tried messaging her on MyBook last night, but she wouldn't answer."

"There's definitely tension between the eighth grad-ers and the seventh graders," Zoe added. "Anna told me that she takes the same bus as Giselle, and usually they sit together, but today Giselle sat with someone else."

I shook my head. "This is all getting so blown out of proportion."

"Hopefully Coach Flores will be back soon and every-thing will be back to normal," Emma said, putting a posi-tive spin on things as usual. "And maybe Coach Valentine will ease up a little bit at today's practice."

But Emma's optimism was no match for Coach Valentine's drill-sergeant coaching style. If anything, he seemed even tougher than usual at practice that day.

"Move it, move it, move it!" he hollered as we did our warm-up laps. Every single Kicks player had made sure to be on time for today's practice!

"You should be glad I'm not making you run in front of a car, girls," he yelled. "Do you know why? Because it would make you tired! Get it, tires, cars?" He started cracking up again. His laugh was just like his voice, gruff and loud.

His laugh was so funny, I couldn't help but laugh along with him, and I noticed a few other girls doing the same.

But then he was right back to drill sergeant. He broke us up into two groups for a one-on-one soccer drill to strengthen our defense and attacks. "Defenders, you have to stay low," he yelled.

I could tell his constant barking was rattling my team-mates' concentration. When we began our scrimmage, I could see that a lot of solid players, like Sarah and Maya, were off their game.

Sarah immediately went offsides. "You need to be aware of where you are at all times!" Coach barked at her.

Maya tripped over the ball, almost taking Anna down with her. "Watch it!" Coach shouted.

He tooted his whistle. "Never mind. We'll run some drills instead. Hey, do you know what a dentist and a soc-cer coach have in common. They both use drills!" Again, he cracked himself up.

I started laughing, and so did Jessi and Emma. "There's

plenty more where that came from, girls," Coach Valentine said. He seemed pleased we were laughing, but not so pleased that he didn't start barking at all of us as soon as the drill started.

We were all missing Coach Flores. I felt burned out as I walked off the field with Jessi when practice was over.

"You know what we need?" I asked Jessi excitedly as an idea popped into my head. "A team building exercise. Just something fun where we can all relax. We haven't done one in ages."

"Fun? Relax? Don't let Coach Valentine hear you saying those words," Jessi joked. "But I agree. We could all use it! What did you have in mind?"

I shrugged. "Let's keep it simple. Maybe we can all go out for pizza after tomorrow's practice."

"That's a great idea," Jessi said. "Count me in!"

"I'll text everybody and invite them!" I said, smiling. Maybe this would be just the thing to cheer everybody up and bring the team together again!

As soon as I climbed into our van, I whipped out my phone and sent a text to everyone on the team.

Pizza after practice tomorrow at Vinnie's?

Before I even got home, my phone began beeping with replies.

Fun! Zoe texted.

U know I'll be there! ☺ came from Jessi.

Only if I can get anchovies on mine, Frida texted back.

"Wow! Are you having a text fest?" My dad joked as he steered the van into our driveway.

"Just some soccer business!" I said as I raced into the house and up the stairs. I kept an eye on my phone all night, waiting to see who was coming. I heard from Emma and Sarah. Later on I got texts from Anna and Olivia, and it wasn't until I was ready to go to bed that I heard back from Brianna. They all said they would come. They were also all seventh graders. Not one of the eighth graders had even bothered to reply. *Some team building exercise this is,* I thought miserably as I turned off my lamp and burrowed under my covers. *More like half-a-team building exercise!*

The next day at school I tried not to think about how none of the eighth graders had texted me back. Instead I tried to concentrate on my schoolwork. But when I got to seventh-period World Civ class, I started thinking of something else: Steven. I hadn't talked to him since he'd brushed me off after the play-off game. I twisted around in my seat, trying to catch a glimpse of him. Not only was he there, but he was staring right at me! I felt a blush creep up my cheeks, but Steven just smiled and waved. I did the same before turning around. *Real smooth, Devin!* I told myself.

After class he was waiting for me in the hallway.

"Hey," he said. "I heard Coach Valentine has taken over until Coach Flores gets back. How's that going?" he asked with a sly grin.

"Ugh!" I groaned. "I feel like I'm in boot camp with a drill sergeant who also moonlights as a comedian."

Steven laughed. "Do you ever feel like you're not sure if you should be saluting him or laughing at one of his jokes?"

"Oh my gosh, totally!" I said. We started walking down the hallway. "So how do you guys put up with him? Do you have any pointers?"

"Yeah, just always do what he says, and you'll have no problem," Steven said, and laughed. "But actually, he's not all bad. He can be really nice, and once our team got into a rhythm with him, we started having a lot of fun at practices. Plus, my skills have improved a lot since I've had him as a coach."

"Your lap running skills?" I joked.

"And my push-up skills." Steven smiled back at me. We were both laughing as we walked into the classroom together.

I saw Cody leaning over Jessi's desk. They were both smiling as Jessi looked up at me. She saw me and winked. The bell rang, and Cody took his seat next to Steven. I slid into the chair next to Jessi's and returned her smile.

"Steven smile!" she whispered to me.

"Cody smile!" I whispered right back. We both laughed. It looked like Steven and Cody had both gotten over their disappointment at losing the play-off game. I was glad for them. Now if only the eighth graders could get over being mad at me!

CHAPTER NINE

Thinking about what Steven had said helped make practice a little more bearable that afternoon. I wanted to improve my soccer skills too, and if Coach Valentine could help me do that, then the hard work was worth it. And if the boys could do it, so could I, right?

Thinking about pizza helped me get through practice too. Even though only the seventh graders were going, I knew it would still be fun. (And also, I loved pizza!)

We ran back into the locker room to change when practice was over. Lately the eighth graders were all changing by the back row of lockers, and the seventh graders were all clumped together by the front door. It almost felt like we were two different teams!

"So, I was thinking, do we have to go to Vinnie's?" Jessi asked as we got changed.

"What's wrong with Vinnie's?" I asked.

"Well, they don't make pineapple pizza, and I'm totally craving that," she answered.

"Mmm, pineapple!" Anna agreed.

I made a face. Back in Connecticut nobody put pineapple on pizza. But in California people put all kinds of strange stuff on it. I liked mine old-school—plain, pepperoni, or sometimes a veggie slice. But that was as crazy as I got.

"Well, where do you want to go?" I asked.

"How about Pizza Kitchen?" Emma suggested.

I shrugged. "That's fine with me. Everybody else okay?"

All of the girls nodded. "Okay, then," I said. "Let's all meet at Pizza Kitchen."

Jessi's mom had agreed to drive me, Frida, Emma, and Zoe, so we all piled into her minivan once we got to the parking lot.

"Mom, we're going to Pizza Kitchen instead," Jessi informed her as she slid into the passenger seat.

Mrs. Dukes smiled. "Oh, good. I need to do some shopping, and that's right next to the market."

A few minutes later we arrived at Pizza Kitchen, a pretty normal-looking pizza parlor in the middle of a strip mall. Brianna, Sarah, Anna, and Olivia had gotten there first and were pushing two tables together so we could all sit in one place.

"Should we get slices or a couple of pizzas?" Brianna asked. "Pizzas are cheaper if we can all agree."

"Pineapple!" yelled Jessi and Frida at the same time.

"Anything but pineapple!" I yelled, and we all started laughing. After we all weighed in, we finally agreed on getting one pineapple pizza and one plain (although Frida was disappointed about not getting her anchovies).

"I'll go put in the order," I said, heading for the counter.

Then the bell on the door jingled, and I turned my head. Grace and Megan were walking in the front door. Grace turned a little bit pink when she saw me, and she and Megan turned their heads and started to whisper. Then they both sat down at the table closest to the door.

Okay, I thought. *So they didn't want to have pizza with us. They're still allowed to have pizza together, right?*

I stepped up to the counter and placed our order, and when I turned around again, more girls were coming through the door. Eight more girls, in fact—the rest of the eighth-grade Kicks!

Maya got a look of shock on her face, and it looked like she was going to say something to me, but Megan quickly pulled her down onto the chair next to her. I went back to my table, where my friends were all talking.

"Can you *believe* it?" Jessi asked.

"They must have thought that we were going to Vinnie's," Frida guessed, "and they planned their own pizza thing here."

Jessi turned and looked right at them. "We should say something."

"No, we shouldn't!" Emma looked anxious.

"Well, what are we supposed to do?" Zoe asked. "Pretend like we don't see them?"

"Of course not," I said. "But Jessi's right. I'm going to ask them about it."

I marched over to their table with Jessi beside me.

"Hi," Jessi said loudly.

"Hey," Grace said with a toss of her blond hair, not looking either of us in the eyes. Next to her Megan just kind of glared at me. The rest of the girls started whispering to one another.

"Did any of you get my texts? About going for pizza as a team?" I asked.

Grace looked uncomfortable. "We planned our own pizza night," she said without answering my question.

"I get that you guys are mad at me," I said. "But why are you taking it out on the other seventh graders? That's not fair."

"Grace is a captain too," Alandra piped up, her eyes flashing. "I don't think you seventh graders get that."

"Yeah, everyone on the team should listen to Grace as much as they do to you," Anjali said.

"Does that mean listening when Grace tells them not to pass the ball to me? Because as a captain I would never tell anyone to do that." I felt my cheeks turning red as I spoke.

"I told you, I never told anyone to do that," Grace said, her voice rising.

"Maybe the eighth graders are the ones who need to listen to you more," Jessi said, her arms crossed in front of her. "Because that's what they've been telling the seventh graders to do. And they're saying it's what you want."

Grace shrugged while Megan shook her head and stood up.

"Whatever," she said. "We need to order our pizza." She walked over to the counter, and Grace followed her.

Jessi and I walked back to our own table. "Unbelievable!" she hissed.

I shook my head. "This is bad. There's no way we can play as a team if we're divided like this."

A server came by and put two pizzas on our table, along with plates, napkins, and pitchers of drinks. The eighth graders had almost ruined my appetite—almost. I couldn't resist the smell of the hot pizza, so I grabbed a slice. Next to me Emma started shaking red pepper flakes on hers.

"Mmm, spicy!" she said, taking a bite.

"What happened?" Frida demanded.

Jessi filled her in.

Anna shook her head. "If Grace wants us to listen to her as captain, she should talk to us as a team at practice. How are we to know what to believe with all these MyBook rumors flying around?"

I groaned. "If only Coach Flores were here. If she had planned this team building exercise, the eighth graders would have come, and maybe we could have put all of this behind us."

Everyone nodded sadly as they chewed their pizza.

"This is a total bummer," Brianna said. "Let's change the subject." She looked down the table at Zoe. "Zoe, I'm so psyched for your bat mitzvah. And I love your theme."

Zoe grinned. "'Fashion Week.' Yeah, I had to do that one!"

"I think I found the cutest dress," Olivia chimed in. "Did you find yours yet?"

"I've narrowed it down to two," Zoe replied. She handed Olivia her phone. "The black one is so beautiful. But the pink one is more fun. What do you think?"

"I like the pink one," Olivia said. She showed the phone to Sarah. "What do you think?"

"Pink," Sarah agreed. "I think black is too harsh for you, Zoe."

Then she scrolled through the photos. "Hey, what's this black one with the fringe? That's really cool."

"I'm getting that one," Frida said.

Zoe sighed and looked at me and Emma. "You know, we really need to get back to Debi's so that you guys can get your dresses."

"I know," I said. "It's just been so hard, with practice and everything, and we've got a game on Saturday. . . ."

Zoe frowned. "You know, I'm starting to wish that we had never made the play-offs," she grumbled.

Nobody said anything right away, and there was an awkward silence at the table.

Emma spoke up first. "Zoe, we all wanted to make the play-offs. I know you don't mean that."

"I don't. It's just—it's getting in the way," she said, looking away from us. "I am totally stressed out. I've got to plan this bat mitzvah, practice soccer, and then there's school besides. It's too much."

"Everything will be fine," Emma promised. "You're a great soccer player; you're, like, an A student; and the party is going to be amazing. I'm even wearing a dress for you."

Zoe smiled a little. "Yeah, that's true."

"And we'll find a way to get to Debi's and get our dresses," I said. "I promise."

"Thanks," Zoe said. She sounded relieved, but her worried look returned when she glanced at the eighth graders. "You know, I invited the whole team to my party. Do you still think they'll come?"

"I hope so," I answered, even though I wasn't sure if they would.

Her question made me upset. I slapped my half-eaten slice onto my plate. Now I had definitely lost my appetite.

Coach Flores was still gone. We weren't working together as a team. And in two days we were facing our rivals, the Panthers, for the title of league champions. I didn't think we had any chance at all of beating them now.

But I didn't tell my teammates that. I was their co-captain, after all, and it was my job to help lead the team, no matter how I felt inside.

I picked up my water glass. "To the Kicks!" I said.

"To the Kicks!" everyone repeated, clicking glasses.

Across the room I could see the eighth graders looking at us. I raised my glass toward them, too, and Megan rolled her eyes.

I tried not to let it get to me. Maybe they weren't going to be team players, but I still could be.

CHAPTER TEN

"Devin, pinch me!" Frida held out her arm to me. We were sitting in the back of my parents' van with Maisie, on our way to the game.

I gave Frida a small pinch.

"Ouch!" she cried, rubbing her arm. "Okay, I'm not dreaming. We're really on our way to the league championship game! But why does the game have to be at the Pinewood field?"

"Well, Pinewood had more wins than us this season, so they get to host the game," I explained.

"You're going to beat Pinewood, right?" Maisie asked.

"I hope so," I replied, my heart beating faster at the thought. "We beat them once before. If we win today, we'll get the division trophy."

"Wow!" Maisie said, her eyes growing wide.

"And if we win this game, we'll have a chance at being state champions," I told her.

"We lost to the Panthers once too," Frida reminded me as she nervously tapped her foot. "I'm really going to need to psych myself up today."

"I was trying to think of a good character for you, but I can't," I said. "Maybe Emma has an idea."

"What are you talking about?" my little sister asked.

"I like to pretend I'm someone else on the soccer field," Frida said. "It's fun. Plus it helps me not be nervous when I'm out there."

Maisie's eyes lit up. "How about a princess?"

"A soccer princess? I don't think so," I said. "Frida needs to be somebody strong and tough for this game."

"But princesses are strong and tough," Maisie protested. "Like Princess Fiona in *Shrek*."

Frida nodded. "You know, that might work. I could be Princess Frida, and the opposing players could be . . . evil goblins!"

"And you're helping Princess Emma to guard the treasure in the tower," I said.

Frida laughed. "Perfect!"

"Can I help?" Maisie asked.

She looked at me with her big brown eyes, and it was one of those times when I remembered how cute she was.

"Sure," I said. "You can be Princess Maisie, and you can send Princess Frida special princess energy from the stands."

Maisie nodded. "I will send you lots of princess energy," she said, her expression serious.

Then we pulled into the parking lot at the Panthers field. They had decorated their stands with purple and gold streamers, and there were big signs everywhere that read, GO PANTHERS! Players from both teams were starting to warm up on opposite sides of the field.

"Look, goblins!" Maisie yelled, pointing at the Panthers players.

Frida laughed. "Your little sister is awesome."

"Yeah, I guess she is," I admitted.

Frida and I ran to join the Kicks on the field. We jogged past a group of Panthers. One of them was a tall girl with her dark hair pulled back into a French braid.

"Hi, Mirabelle," I said.

I guess you could have called Mirabelle a frenemy of mine. She was on the Kicks when I first joined, but now she played for the Panthers.

Mirabelle nodded. "Hey, Devin," she said coolly, and then she and the Panthers jogged off.

"Well, that was surprisingly drama-free," Frida said. "I was expecting some trash talk."

"I think we have a truce with Mirabelle," I said. "She sort of took our side when the Rams were trying to sabotage us."

Frida nodded. "Well, the Rams were trying to frame Mirabelle for everything they did, so that makes sense."

"Anyway, I'm glad she's being cool," I said. "That's one less thing to worry about today."

Coach Valentine had the girls dribbling around cones that he had set up, and Frida and I lined up behind Emma to wait for our turn.

"Oh my gosh!" Emma said. "Did you get that e-mail from Coach Flores last night?"

Frida and I nodded. Coach had sent a message to everyone on the team.

To all my Kicks:

I want to apologize for leaving so suddenly. My dad is in the hospital, and it was pretty serious for a while, but it looks like he's doing better now. I won't make it to tomorrow's game, but I want you to know that I'm with you all in spirit. You guys have worked hard for this. Do your best, help one another out, and no matter what happens, know that I am superproud of you.

Coach Flores

"I totally cried when I read it!" Emma said.

"Me too," Frida admitted.

"I hope the eighth graders read that part about helping one another out," I said, eyeing Grace as she dribbled through the cones.

"Of course they did," Emma said. "Don't worry, Devin. They're not going to do anything to mess up the game for us."

I wish I could say that Emma was right. But from the start of the game, it was clear that the eighth graders were still holding a grudge.

Coach Valentine had Grace in the midfield with Maya, Taylor, and Jessi—the only seventh grader on the line. He started me, Zoe, and Megan as forwards, just like Coach Flores usually did.

The Panthers won the toss and chose to receive first, but Megan quickly intercepted the ball from them. As she dribbled down the field, two Panthers charged her.

"Megan, over here!" I yelled. I was only about ten feet away, and she had a clear shot.

But Megan ignored me. She kicked the ball to Grace, who must have been fifty feet away. One of the Panthers swept in and kicked it before Grace could get to it. The Panthers player made a beeline for our goal, but our defensive line was ready for her.

"Princess power!" Frida yelled, kicking the ball away. One of the Panthers looked at Frida like she was nuts, and I had to laugh. If acting like this hadn't made Frida a much better player, I would have been embarrassed. But now I was used to her tearing up the soccer field as a vampire, alien, and lots of other crazy characters. Whatever worked!

Taylor got the ball from Frida, and she could have easily passed it to Jessi. But she passed it to Maya instead, and one of the Panthers blocked it. That was how it went the whole first half. The eighth graders refused to pass to any of the seventh graders. Jessi started to get angry about it.

"Come on, over here!" she yelled at one point when Taylor had the ball. She could have easily passed to Jessi, but she just ignored her, and one of the Panthers kicked the ball right from under Taylor's feet.

"I was right there!" Jessi yelled as she raced past Taylor down the field, but Taylor didn't reply.

To make matters worse, the Panthers offense was on fire. They kept getting the ball down by our goal, and Emma made some great saves. But then Emma kicked the ball away from the goal, and one of the Panthers strikers kicked it right back. It whizzed past Emma into the goal.

"Sorry!" she called out.

"It's okay!" I called back.

The Panthers scored again when one of their players dribbled right between Sarah and Anjali until she was just six feet from the goal. Then she sent it skidding superfast across the grass, and Emma couldn't catch it in time.

When the half ended, the Panthers were winning, 2–0. I couldn't help noticing a satisfied smile on Mirabelle's face as she jogged off the field.

Coach Valentine was pretty upset.

"What are you girls doing out there?" he barked, his face turning red. "I've seen you play better than this! It's like you've forgotten how to play! Grace! Devin! What is going on with this team?"

I looked right at Grace. Her cheeks were pink, and she looked uncomfortable.

"We'll do better, Coach," she said.

"Yes we will, Coach," I added quickly.

Coach shook his head. "It makes me wonder how you girls got this far and my boys are sitting at home right now," he said. "I'm gonna figure out a lineup for the second half. Now I want you guys to stretch out."

Coach Valentine's words really stung. He didn't think we were as good as the boys, or that we deserved to be there! Even more than winning, I wanted to prove him wrong—and I knew what I had to do.

I walked up to Grace, who was whispering with Megan and Giselle.

"Grace, can I talk to you a minute?" I asked.

Grace looked from Megan to Giselle, who both shrugged. "I guess," Grace said reluctantly.

She and I walked over to the sidelines. "Listen, I know this all started with you guys mad at me about that newspaper article," I began. "And I'm sorry about that. But it's gone too far. We really need to start working together or we're going to lose this game."

Grace bit her lip and brushed a strand of blond hair away from her face. "We're not trying to lose," she said.

"Maybe not, but that's what is going to happen if we keep playing with only half a team," I said. "It's like what Coach Flores said. We have to help one another. We have to play as a team."

Grace looked over at Coach Valentine. "I wish Coach Flores were here."

"I do too," I said. "But she's not. And Coach Valentine

thinks we stink compared to his precious boys' team. We need to prove him wrong."

Grace nodded.

"So are we good?" I asked.

"I guess," Grace said hesitantly. "For now."

It was better than nothing. "Then let's do this," I said.

Grace and I jogged back to the team. Grace clapped her hands.

"So, listen up!" she called out. (Grace was always pretty quiet, but she could be loud when she needed to be.) "We need to work together as a team out there, just like Coach Flores said. We've got to help one another."

She looked right at Megan and the other eighth graders. "That means we're all in this together. Got it?"

Megan kind of frowned, but most of the other eighth graders nodded.

"Got it!" everyone shouted.

Coach walked up to us. "I need you guys to play like you mean it!" he said. "I know you've got it in you. Brianna, Devin, Zoe, you're forwards. Olivia, Gabriela, Maya, Alandra, you're midfield. Frida, Sarah, Anjali, defense. Emma, I want you back on goal. But, defense, you need to work harder for her. Got it?"

"Got it, Coach!" everyone shouted again.

Grace thrust her hand in front of her, and we each slapped a hand on top of hers.

"Goooooooo, Kicks!"

CHAPTER ELEVEN

My heart was pumping fast as I ran out onto the field at the start of the second half. Now that things with the eighth graders were mostly settled, I started to think about what it might mean to win this game.

If we beat the Panthers, then we would win our division. The Kentville Kangaroos would be division champs. That would be amazing.

After that we'd go on to the early rounds of the state championships. The Kentville Kangaroos would actually have a shot at being California state champs. That would be even *more* amazing.

But first we had to beat the Panthers, and we were down by two goals.

The ref's whistle blew, and we charged into the half. I noticed that Coach Valentine had taken off the field most of the girls who hadn't been passing to the seventh graders. Had he figured out what was going on?

We still had eighth graders on the field, though, and they must have listened to Grace, because suddenly we were working like a team again. Gabriela got control of the ball and passed it to Olivia. Olivia avoided a Panthers midfielder by passing the ball to Alandra. Alandra took it down the field and then shot it to Brianna. Brianna shot it right into the goal—and just like that, we had scored our first goal!

"Princess power!" I heard Maisie yell from the stands, and the rest of the Kicks fans went wild.

I high-fived Brianna and we jogged down the field. The Panthers quickly made their way to our goal, but our defense gave them a good fight.

"Take that, goblins!" Frida cried as she kicked a ball away from one of the Panthers strikers.

The second half moved really fast, and Coach kept switching up the players. He brought Grace, Taylor, Megan, and Jessi back in, but he never took me out— something I was secretly proud of.

But the best thing was that Grace and Taylor passed the ball to me and Zoe a few times. Megan, Zoe, and I kept getting close to the Panthers goal, but the defense kept getting control of the ball.

Then we got lucky. One of the Panthers kicked the ball out of bounds, and Grace threw it in. I was right on it, but I hadn't gotten far when one of the Panthers ran right up to me.

That's when I spotted Megan right by the goal, and I

passed the ball to her. The kick bounced up at the end, but Megan kneed it—right into the goal!

The score was tied 2–2!

"Way to go, Megan!" I yelled, high-fiving her, and Megan slapped my hand back.

Both the Kicks and the Panthers tried to break the tie, but by the time the second half ended, neither of us had scored. During the regular season, it was okay for a game to end in a tie. But this was a division championship game, so there would be a tiebreaker. I ran off the field with the other Kicks, and we gathered around Coach Valentine.

"The league director has specified that in the event of a tie, there'll be a shoot-out," he explained.

"Like in the Wild West?" Emma asked.

Coach sighed. "No, not like in the Wild West. It's a penalty shoot-out. The ball is set up at the twelve-yard line, and you'll take turns shooting. Each team gets three shots on goal. The team that scores the most during the shootout wins the game. Emma, I want you on goal."

Emma turned a little pale. "So there's no defenders?"

"No defenders," Coach Valentine said flatly.

"Emma, you can do this," I said. "Remember, we've done shoot-out drills before. You were great."

"Devin, Megan, Grace, you're shooting for us, in that order," he said. "Any questions?"

"Which team goes first?" I asked. I didn't mind going first for my team, but going first for the whole thing— well, that would be a little scary.

"We'll do a coin toss," he said. "Come on. Let's get out there."

Emma, Grace, Megan, and I followed Coach Valentine to the middle of the field. The Panthers coach was there with four Panthers—and one of them was Mirabelle. I wasn't surprised; Mirabelle was a great player.

The ref flipped a coin. "Panthers will shoot first," the ref told us.

"Shooters, line up behind the penalty mark," the ref instructed. "Panthers will get the first shot, then the Kicks, and we'll keep alternating."

Emma ran in to the goal area. She was usually pretty confident, but she looked a little nervous. The ref set the ball up on the penalty mark, and Mirabelle stepped up to it.

"Goalie, are you ready?" the ref yelled to Emma, and she nodded. Then the ref nodded at Mirabelle. "Whenever you want."

Mirabelle looked as confident as always. She ran up to the ball and kicked it hard, sending it skidding across the grass. Emma should have been able to get it, but when she ran for it, she tripped and fell, and the ball skidded past her hands and into the goal.

"One point for the Panthers," the ref said, and Mirabelle jumped up and let out a loud "Whoop!" The Panthers fans went wild.

Emma looked shaken as she jogged away from the goal and the Panthers goalie took her place.

"Don't worry, Emma. You'll get the next one!" I called out.

"Devin, you're up," Coach Valentine said.

I jogged up to the penalty mark and took a deep breath. I could feel my stomach starting to flip-flop, and I tried to hold back the nerves, but to be honest, I was starting to freak out. There must have been a hundred people in the stands, and they were all watching me. I took a deep breath as the crowd quieted down.

Then Maisie yelled out, "Princess power!"

I was too nervous to be embarrassed, but then it hit me—that's how Frida stayed focused, by pretending to be someone else. I wasn't just Devin, seventh grader about to kick a ball in front of a hundred people. I was Princess Devin, goblin fighter.

I know it sounds silly, but imagining that I was Princess Devin really did take my mind off being nervous. I eyed the Panthers goalie, who was planted firmly in the middle of the net, her hands on her knees.

I ran up to the ball and then kicked with all my might, aiming for the left side of the goal. It soared up across the field and whizzed right over the goalie's head as she jumped for it.

The ref blew his whistle to signify the goal, and then I heard the Kicks fans go wild. Grace and Megan both hugged me, and I felt like I was on top of the whole world. But the shoot-out wasn't over yet.

One of the Panthers took the next shot, and Emma

dove for it, but it slipped through her fingers. Panthers 2, Kicks 1. Megan shot for the Kicks next, and her kick went a little crazy. For a second it looked like it might miss the goal, but it shot in at the last minute, and the goalie missed it. Panthers 2, Kicks 2.

Emma took the goal for the last time. I was worried that she might be totally nervous after letting the first two get past her, but she looked really determined. When the last Panthers player took her shot, it veered to the right. Emma ran after it—and caught it in both hands.

"Woo-hoo! Emma!" Grace and Megan and I yelled, and I could hear the Kicks fans cheering too.

Emma ran up to us. Now it was all up to Grace. The shoot-out score was still 2–2. If Grace got this goal, the Kicks would win the championship.

"You can do it, Grace!" I yelled as Grace jogged up to the penalty mark.

A deadly quiet came over the Panthers field. I could imagine how Grace must have been feeling. So much pressure! I was glad Coach Valentine hadn't picked me to go last.

But I understood why he had chosen Grace. She looked cool and calm, like she always did. It was one of the things that made her a great captain. I held my breath as she kicked the ball and watched it soar at rocket speed toward the goal.

The Panthers goalie gave it her best, but Grace's ball was just too fast. The Panthers player didn't have a chance.

The ball zoomed past her and bounced against the back of the net.

For a second I couldn't believe it. Then Emma was jumping up and down and shaking me like crazy. The Kicks ran out onto the field.

Jessi ran up to me and practically knocked me down.

"We did it!" she shrieked. "The Kicks win the league championship!"

CHAPTER TWELVE

"Goooooooooo, Kicks!"

The whole Kicks team—all nineteen of us—had taken over Pizza Kitchen. The seventh graders were still at one table, and the eighth graders were at another, but at least this time they weren't across the room. Some of our parents were scattered around at other tables too. We all had a lot to celebrate.

"To Grace!" Taylor cried, standing up and holding out her glass of water. "For her game-winning kick!"

Everybody clinked glasses and cheered. Then Jessi stood up.

"Don't forget Devin's kick," she said, and I saw Taylor look at Megan and make a face.

"And Megan," I said, quickly standing up too. "And the whole team! We all did it together."

We all clicked glasses again, and I sat down. The eighth graders started huddling together and whispering, and it struck me that even though we had played like a team on the field, we still didn't feel like the old Kicks. Not yet.

"We should text Coach Flores!" Zoe said, and she quickly started typing into her phone. "She's going to be so happy."

"Do it!" Emma urged.

Zoe sent a quick text, and things settled down when the servers brought a bunch of pizzas to the table. I grabbed a broccoli slice and wolfed it down really fast. I hadn't realized how hungry I was.

"Devin, I can't believe how calm you were out there," Zoe said. "I would have been freaking."

I grinned. "Well, it was all thanks to Princess power."

"Oh my gosh! I did the same thing too," Emma said. "After I let those first two goals go past, I thought I was going to lose it. But then I looked at Frida on the sidelines, and I thought, 'Well, I could be Princess Emma, trying to keep the evil goblins from the goal.' And it worked!"

Jessi groaned. "Does this mean that all of you are going to be acting like drama queens out there every game? Because I don't think I could handle that."

"Don't worry," I said. "It was extreme shoot-out circumstances."

"I don't know," Emma said, grinning at Frida. "It was kind of fun."

Brianna was busy scrolling through her phone. "So I

guess this means practice all next week, right? I'm going to have to move my violin lesson. And try to get into a different dance class. And then there's that chess club tournament." She frowned.

Zoe suddenly looked miserable. "How am I going to get ready for my bat mitzvah if we have practice all next week?"

"We'll help you," Emma said. "There's no practice tomorrow. We could come over tomorrow. Right, guys?"

"Sure," I said. "I just need to ask my mom."

Zoe looked relieved. "That would be so nice. Thanks!"

Suddenly Jessi nudged me with her elbow. "Look who it is."

I turned toward the door and saw Cody and Steven walk in. They came right to our table.

"Hey, we were looking for you guys," Cody said.

"You were?" I asked, but Jessi didn't seem surprised. She was way calmer about the whole hanging-out-with-boys thing than I was.

Steven smiled at me. "We heard about the game. Congratulations."

"Yeah, that's awesome," Cody said.

Jessi looked at me and raised an eyebrow, and I knew what she meant. It was nice that the boys weren't acting all bummed out about losing anymore.

"So, we're going to the mall later," Cody said. "You want to meet us there?"

"Sure," Jessi answered.

"Um, yeah, I guess," I said. I mean, I liked the mall, and Steve and Cody were nice, so what was the big deal, right? "I just have to ask my . . . Mom!"

My mom and Jessi's mom suddenly appeared at our table.

"We just wanted to make sure you girls were enjoying your pizza," Mom said. Then she turned to the boys. "Hello. I'm Devin's mom. Are you friends of Devin's and Jessi's?"

My cheeks turned pink. I had talked to Mom and Dad about Steven a few times, but they had never met him.

"Well, they're—um, I mean—" I stammered.

Jessi jumped in. "This is Cody, and this is Steven," she said, pointing. "They're on the boys' team. We're going to meet them at the mall later. Is that okay?" She looked at her mom.

Mrs. Dukes and my mom looked at each other.

"What time?" Mrs. Dukes asked.

"Around four," Cody replied. "Just for a little while."

"Dad can drop you off at four, and pick you up at six," Mom said to me. Then she turned to the boys. "How did you boys get here? Are your parents outside? I'd love to meet them."

"Me too," added Mrs. Dukes.

Steven smiled. "Sure, my mom's outside."

Mom and Mrs. Dukes walked away with Cody and Steven, and I turned to Jessi.

"I cannot believe that just happened," I said.

"Captain Kiss strikes again!" Frida yelled, and then she started giggling like crazy.

Jessi shook her head. "Do you think our moms will always be like this?"

I nodded. "Definitely!"

When the pizza party ended, I went home to shower and change. I put on my favorite blue shirt with butterflies on it and a denim skirt and my blue flip-flops. Then Dad took me to pick up Jessi.

I was expecting Dad to tease us in the car, but he just put on the classic rock station and started humming along.

Well, why would he tease us? I thought. *We're just going to the mall. It's not like it's a date or anything.*

And then it hit me. Cody and Steven had asked Jessi and me to go to the mall with them. Just the four of us. It *was* a date! A double date!

Panicked, I turned and looked at Jessi in the backseat.

"What's wrong?" Jessi asked, noticing the expression on my face.

I didn't want to say anything out loud, because I didn't want my dad to hear. So I took out my phone and texted her.

So I just realized that this is a double date. Why didn't u tell me?

What do u mean? Jessi asked. Of course it's a double date.

But I thought we were just going to the mall, I typed.

That's a date! Jessi texted back.

That's when I noticed that we were at a stoplight—and my dad was looking right at the phone in my lap.

"Nobody says this has to be a date," he said.

I groaned and put my head in my hands. "This is so embarrassing."

"Listen, it's not a big deal," Dad said. "In fact, it shouldn't be, especially at your age. Just hang out and have fun."

"Exactly!" Jessi piped up.

"But what if *they* think it's a double date?" I asked.

"Then just tell them your dad said you're not allowed to date until you're sixteen," Dad said.

"Sixteen!" I wailed, but part of me was glad he had said that.

Dad pulled up to the mall entrance. "Where are they meeting you?"

"By the arcade," Jessi replied. "Cody texted me."

"Okay, then," Dad said. "Don't leave the mall. Keep your phone on. And I'll meet you right here at six."

I gave him a kiss on the cheek. "Bye, Dad."

Jessi and I headed into the mall and up the escalator. We found Cody and Steven hanging outside the arcade, just like Jessi had said.

"Hey," Cody said, nodding.

"Hey," Jessi said.

Steven smiled at me. "Hi."

"Hi," I said back.

Then nobody said anything for a minute, and I worried

that "hey" and "hi" were going to be all anybody could say all night. Then Jessi broke the ice.

"I am undefeated on this thing!" she said, running over to the Dance Party! machine by the front of the arcade. It was one of those arcade games where music played and you had to follow the arrows on a screen and step on the arrows that lit up on the floor.

I nodded. "She is seriously awesome. I've seen her."

Jessi slid a dollar into the machine. "Watch."

Music started pumping from the machine, and Jessi began to dance, her feet moving like lightning on the pad. A bunch of other kids gathered around to watch.

When the song ended, she jumped off the pad. "And that is how it's done!" she said, grinning.

Cody jumped up. "Oh, yeah?" he asked, putting a dollar into the machine.

Cody was pretty good, I had to admit—but not as good as Jessi. When he finished, his score was fifty thousand points less than hers.

Jessi smiled at him. "Don't worry about it. I'm hard to beat."

"My turn!" Steven yelled, and he put his dollar in. The music started, and Steven started . . . well, it wasn't exactly dancing. He waved his arms around and he stomped on the arrows but never the right ones, and in the middle of the song he tripped over his own feet and had to grab on to the bars on either side of the platform to keep from falling.

It took me a minute to realize that Steven wasn't a terrible dancer—he was just having fun. I started cracking up, and then I noticed that Jessi was laughing so hard, she was doubled over.

"Dude! You stink!" Cody yelled over the music.

"I'm awesome!" Steven yelled back.

Finally the music ended, and Steven jumped off the machine.

"The master," he said, bowing. "Your turn, Devin."

I shook my head. "No way. I can't follow any of that." I nodded toward the basketball machine. "Come on. I'm really good at that one."

So I made ten perfect shots in the basketball machine, and we played some more games, and then we were thirsty and we got lemonade, and before I knew it, it was time to go. Cody and Steven didn't say anything about dating at all. Basically we just hung out and had fun.

Sometimes I hated it when my dad was right. This time I was really glad that he was.

CHAPTER THIRTEEN

"Hit the lights!" I called.

"On it!" Jessi yelled back.

The bedroom that Zoe shared with her sister went dark before her laptop lit up the room. When we'd gotten to Zoe's house, Jessi had confiscated Zoe's laptop and uploaded the video from her phone onto it without telling Zoe what it was. We wanted it to be a surprise.

Frida's smiling face filled the screen. She was wearing the black fringe dress that Zoe had picked out for her, and she turned from side to side, modeling it for the camera.

Zoe clapped her hands together. "You went to Debi's!"

"Surprise!" Emma cried. "We all went there this morning for our fittings, and Jessi took a video with her phone so you could see how they looked on us."

Emma appeared on the screen next, wearing the long, shimmering dress. She tried to twirl around but stumbled and had to grab on to the mirror next to her to keep from falling. You could hear the rest of us giggling and Debi's loud groan of frustration in the background.

"That Debi needs to chill!" Jessi said. "Hey, I wonder if she's married. We could introduce her to Coach Valentine."

We all cracked up.

"Actually, it wouldn't work. As dorky as it is, at least Coach Valentine has a sense of humor. Debi doesn't!" I said, just as I saw myself on the video. The blue dress with silver flowers was the prettiest I had ever worn. I smiled at the camera, my hands on my hips.

Next up was Jessi, looking so cute in the sparkly silver dress. She had given me her phone so I could take the video. Jessi posed confidently for the camera, a huge grin on her face.

"You guys look so awesome!" Zoe was all smiles.

"It's all thanks to you," I told her. "You should be a stylist. The dresses you picked out for all of us are amazingly perfect!"

Zoe blushed. "It was really fun."

"And you're really good at it!" Emma added. "Now you don't have to worry about our dresses anymore. So you can cross it off your bat mitzvah to-do list!"

Zoe sighed. "That's great, because I accidentally added another thing to my list. Check this out."

Zoe held up her phone, showing us a picture of her in a one-shoulder dress. The top was black-and-white sequined stripes flowing into a fluffy black tulle skirt.

"That dress definitely has the drama factor," Frida said.

"Now I have three dresses I can't decide between!" Zoe said. "My mom and I went back to Debi's last night. I was going to only try on the pink and black dresses so I could finally make up my mind. But then I saw this one and I couldn't resist trying it on."

"It's supercute!" Emma said. "But I think I still like the pink one the best."

Zoe frowned. "I've got to make a decision soon!" She sighed, but then her face brightened. "Thanks for coming to help today. I thought we could all work on my party favors. Everything is set up in the craft room. Let's go!"

Zoe lived in one of those ranch houses with two levels. We walked downstairs through the family room to a small room next to the laundry room.

"Dad wanted this room for a man cave, but with four daughters, he got outvoted," Zoe joked as she opened the door. Three walls were all shelves, filled with baskets, books, binders, and jars; everything was perfectly organized. The fourth wall had a workstation with a computer and a sewing machine.

In the middle of the room was a square table with six chairs around it. Round black-and-white striped boxes sat on the table along with brown paper bags, hot-glue guns, and other crafting items.

"My party favor theme for the girl guests is Beauty in a Box," Zoe explained. "I'm going to fill these boxes with bubble bath, makeup, a pedicure kit, the kind of things to pamper yourself and feel pretty with. My sisters and I already finished the gift boxes for the boys," she said, gesturing to a row of blue-and-white striped boxes on the shelf. "They're filled with sunglasses and body spray. I still wanted to keep the fashion theme for the boys, but it was hard to figure out what to give them!" She pulled a finished black-and-white box off a shelf. It had a hot-pink bow on the lid and rhinestones all around. "So would you guys help me sparkle up the girls' boxes, like this? I've got everything. We've just got to hot-glue them on."

"Fun!" Emma said: "But I have to warn you, once I hot-glued my fingers together."

"Um, Emma, I was there," Jessi said, and grinned. "You hot-glued your fingers to your cousin's dog, remember?"

Emma laughed. "First I hot-glued my fingers together. Then I tried to wipe them off. I mistook Daisy for a fluffy white towel! My aunt Jae was so mad."

We all giggled as we started working on the boxes. I glued the pink bow on top of the box and admired my work. I wasn't a real crafty person, but it was fun and actually kind of relaxing.

"I can't believe my bat mitzvah is less than a week away!" Zoe said as we worked. "I feel like there's still so much I have to do. And now we have the regional game that day."

I nodded. "The game is in Brightville at eleven a.m. I mapped it out. It's about an hour away."

"An hour?" Zoe's face crumpled. "So we'll have a long drive *and* a game. Perfect."

"We'll be fine," Emma said cheerfully as she glued a rhinestone onto the box and not her fingers. "Don't worry."

"But I have the temple service at four o'clock, before the party," Zoe said, looking panicked. "So we'll have to rush home and get changed in a hurry if we want to be on time."

"Well, if we get back home by two, you'll still have a couple of hours to get ready," Frida offered. "It's like changing in between scenes when you're in a play. It's hectic but fun. And a huge adrenaline rush besides."

Zoe sighed. "I guess it'll be okay," she said nervously. "I'm so glad now that we decided to do the sunset service instead of a morning one. Then it would have been *totally* ruined. But it's still going to be crazy!"

Jessi and I exchanged worried glances, but I didn't know what to say to make Zoe feel better. She was right. It was going to be a hectic day.

Just then Zoe's mom came into the room.

"Hi, girls," she said. "Thanks for helping Zoe with the party favors. I just got back from picking up the red carpet runner. Do you all want to see?"

Zoe's frown was quickly replaced by a smile. "Yes!" We followed into the family room, where a plush red carpet was rolled out across the floor.

Zoe gave a squeal of delight. "Thanks, Mom!" she said as she gave her mom a big hug. "It's perfect." She turned to us. "It's for all of the party guests to walk down, just like at a big-name designer's fashion show!"

Mrs. Quinlan smiled. "I'm glad you like it. You all must be hungry. I'll go fix you some snacks," she said, heading back upstairs.

Frida immediately stepped onto the carpet and struck a pose, one hand on her hip, her head turned and an eyebrow arched. Then she began strutting down the carpet, pretending to wave at her fans. "No autographs, please," she said, putting a hand dramatically on her forehead.

"Wait! We need music." Jessi pulled her phone out of her pocket and pressed a button. A song with a bouncy beat filled the air.

"Perfect!" Jessi said. She walked down the carpet, her hips swaying back and forth to the music. When she got to the end, she pretended to stop and pose for a photographer. She whirled around and looked over her shoulder, smiling prettily.

I took my turn afterward, walking down the carpet with a hand on my hip, as if I were a model on a runway. But halfway through I burst out laughing.

"I feel so silly!" I said.

"You've got to be fierce!" Frida told me. "Work it like you own it!"

I tried sucking in my cheeks and arching my eyebrows, hoping that looked fierce, but everyone just started laughing instead.

"My turn!" Emma said.

But Jessi stopped her. "You should practice with your heels on. That's what you were wearing at Debi's this morning."

Emma grinned sheepishly. "That's why I tripped on the video. I've got them in my bag. Wait a sec." She disappeared up the stairs toward Zoe's room.

"My mom is letting me wear heels for the first time for the party," Jessi told us while Emma was gone. "They are supercute! The heel isn't that high, though."

I shook my head. "I just want to be comfortable. I'll stick to flats, or better yet, flip-flops!"

Emma came back down the stairs, carrying the gold, sparkly heels like they were a snake about to bite her. She held the heels by the tips of her fingers, as far away from her body as possible.

"They are too cute!" Zoe gushed. "The heel isn't that big."

"Yeah, but I can trip in my bare feet," Emma reminded her.

Emma sat on the bottom step and put the shoes on. "Here goes nothing," she said as she stood up. Emma was pretty tall, but in the heels she looked even taller. She took a few cautious steps, and her face brightened. "Not too bad," she said as she stepped onto the plush red rug.

Jessi held up her phone, and the music filled the air. Emma struck a pose and then launched down the carpet, bouncing to the beat as she went.

"Go, Emma!" Frida hooted, while Zoe and I clapped.

"I'm doing it!" she cried. In her excitement she began to walk even faster. Her heel caught the edge of the carpet, and a look of panic filled her face.

"Help!" she called, her arms flailing wildly in the air.

Zoe and I rushed over to catch her, but it was too late. Emma sat in a crumpled heap on the red carpet, her face buried in her hands and her body shaking.

"Emma! Are you okay?" I leaned over her, worried.

Emma looked up. Her face was bright red, but she wasn't crying. She was laughing!

"I guess my career as a model is over before it even started," she said between giggles.

Zoe sat down next to her and put an arm around her. "Maybe we should go shopping for some flats."

"And a helmet and some elbow pads," Emma said. "I think I need safety gear on at all times."

We started laughing hysterically.

"See, Zoe," Emma said after she caught her breath. "You don't have to worry about Saturday. No matter what happens, we'll have a good time."

I laughed. "But bring some safety gear just in case!"

CHAPTER FOURTEEN

I was still smiling when my mom picked me up at Zoe's house later that afternoon. We'd finished the party favor boxes, and they looked great. Zoe seemed a lot more relaxed about the game and her bat mitzvah on Saturday, although she was still obsessing about all the last-minute details.

"You look like you had a good time," my mom remarked as I got into the van.

I told her all about Emma's adventures in heels. "But I'm going to stick to flats. Or how about a pair of sparkly flip-flops?"

My mom laughed. "You've been living in flip-flops ever since we moved to California."

She was right. I had a pair in just about every color.

"I have something I want to talk to you about," my mom said, in that serious tone of voice she usually reserved for when I was in trouble. I racked my brains. I couldn't think of anything wrong I had done! But I was off the hook. Sort of.

"That reporter from the *Kentville Chronicle*, Cassidy Vale, called while you were at Zoe's," my mom said.

"Ugh!" I said angrily. "What did she want?"

"She wanted to interview you before the regional play-off game," Mom said. "What do you think?"

I groaned. "No way! She never even admitted she was wrong. What if she gets my words mixed up again? I can't risk it."

Mom nodded. "I understand. But your dad and I were talking about it. What if you wrote a letter to the newspaper? That way it could be in your own words and you could keep a copy, so if anything got printed wrong, you would have proof."

Hmmmm. That was an interesting idea. "Kind of like a letter to the editor?" I asked.

"Exactly," Mom said.

I smiled. "I'll write it as soon as we get home!"

As soon as we pulled into the driveway, I was out of the van like a shot. I raced upstairs and sat down at my computer, eager to finally get my side of the story in print. When I wrote a paper for class, sometimes I felt like I was having a staring contest with my computer screen. I couldn't think of what to say and I'd just look at my screen, hoping the words would magically appear. But I didn't have that problem at all today. The words came out in a rush, almost faster than I could type them.

Dear *Kentville Chronicle,*

My name is Devin Burke, and I am a seventh grader at Kentville Middle School. But more important, I am one of the Kicks. And the Kicks will be playing in the regional play-offs against the Brightville Bolts this Saturday.

When I first joined the Kangaroos and became a member of the Kicks, the team's record was not great. But we all worked together as a team, each and every one of us, and we worked hard to get where we are today, which is the Kicks' first play-off season in almost twenty years. We did it together, and every single person on the team made it happen.

In an article that ran earlier in the *Chronicle*, I was misquoted as saying "I don't know where my team would be without me." What I really said was, "I don't know where I'd be without my team." I want to say it again: I don't know where I'd be without my team. They've shown me that anything is possible if you work hard. And we've all become friends. In fact, we're more like a family. And whether we win or lose, we'll always be a team.

Go, Kicks!

Sincerely,
Devin Burke

I let out a big sigh as I finished. It felt good to get that off my chest. I would ask my mom to read it before I e-mailed it to the newspaper. I only hoped the *Chronicle* would print it!

The next day after school we had practice—still without Coach Flores. But I was strangely getting used to Coach Valentine. His method of coaching might have been strict, but it had its upsides too.

"Hustle, hustle, hustle!" he yelled as we were dribbling through the cones. I used to jump every time he yelled, but now it just made me go faster.

He blew sharply into his whistle. "Good work, girls. Hit the locker room. Do any of you have math homework tonight? Don't worry if you do. Soccer players always do great in math. That's because they always know how to use their heads!"

Coach Valentine started laughing, and a lot of the girls joined in. We could tell now that if Coach started joking around, he was happy about how we were playing.

We all piled into the locker room, chatting away. I noticed the eighth graders had definitely thawed toward the seventh graders since the game against the Panthers. But once we got into the locker room, we were segregated again. The eighth graders all clustered in the back row, while the seventh graders stayed at the lockers closest to the door. We still weren't totally back to normal. I closed my eyes and made a wish that the *Chronicle* would print my letter—and soon!

Zoe changed in record time. "I've got to run. Today is the day I have to finalize the party menu. Bye!" she cried as she dashed out of the room.

"Now you see her, now you don't," Jessi said, and laughed. "She's fast on the field and fast when she has to go party planning."

"Guys!" Emma slammed her locker door shut, and it made me jump. "I totally just thought of something. We've got to get Zoe a bat mitzvah present!"

"My mom was going to pick something up," Jessi said. I nodded. My mom had said she would take care of it too.

Frida said, "My mom said we would give her money."

Emma frowned. "Zoe is one of our best friends. We should get her a special gift. What if we all chip in together and pick out something meaningful?"

"I like that idea," I said, agreeing with Emma. "Zoe keeps talking about how she wants to remember this day forever. We should get her something she can keep forever, so it will always remind her of her bat mitzvah."

"And of us!" Jessi said. "I like that idea. I'm in!"

"We could all go to the mall now," Emma suggested. "I can ask my mom to drive us."

We all ran out to the parking lot to get the okay from our parents, and soon we were in Emma's mother's SUV heading to the mall.

"I think that's a really sweet thought," Mrs. Kim said of our plan. "How about jewelry? That's something she could keep forever."

So when Mrs. Kim dropped us off at the mall entrance, we decided to check out some of the jewelry stores first.

The first store we walked into had some really cute stuff, but it was all costume jewelry.

"This won't last forever." Frida held up a pretty, sparkly bracelet. "In fact, I think it might turn Zoe's wrist green."

"Since we're all chipping in, we can afford to get something nice and more expensive," Emma said as we headed back out into the mall. "Let's try this store!"

The next store we tried was way too fancy. I gulped at the price tags on some of the items. A thin saleswoman with a pointy nose came over to us. "Can I help you?" she said, looking down her nose at us and fixing us with a snooty stare.

I grew flustered. "How much is that?" I asked, pointing randomly at a tiara that sat in a locked glass case.

"That is a vintage Cartier diamond tiara," the woman said with a sniff. "It sells for more than one hundred thousand dollars. I doubt you could afford it."

But Frida sniffed right back at her. "A hundred thousand dollars? Our friend is worth more than that. Come, girls, let's find a jewelry shop with finer-quality items. And with better service." She said it like she was pretending to be Princess Frida again. She swept out of the store like royalty, and we followed her, giggling.

Jessi laughed. "I wonder if that woman was related to Debi."

Emma's eyes were wide. "I can't believe you stood up to that saleslady like that, Frida."

"It's no problem," Frida said with a smile. "I just called upon my inner diva. She's always there, waiting to get out!"

We laughed as we walked into another store. I glanced around. This one had some cute things, and it didn't seem too expensive or too cheap.

An older saleswoman with curly brown hair streaked with gray came over to us. "Are you looking for something in particular, girls?" she asked with a smile.

"We're looking for a bat mitzvah gift for a friend," Emma explained. "We want to give her something really special."

"I can show you items that are popular bat mitzvah gifts to start," the saleswoman suggested. "And we can go from there."

First she showed us necklaces of the Star of David, a six-pointed star that was a symbol of the Jewish people. The necklaces were really nice, especially one that was lined with diamonds.

"Oh, pretty," Emma said, her eyes growing wide at the sight of the shiny star.

"But anyone can give Zoe a Star of David," Frida complained. "We need something that would only come from us."

"Do you have any hobbies or things you like to do together?" the saleswoman asked.

"She loves fashion," Jessi said. "Zoe is a true fashionista."

The woman nodded. "So something fashion forward."

She showed us some necklaces and bracelets. They were all really beautiful, but nothing clicked.

"Wait!" I said. I couldn't believe I hadn't thought of this before. "What about soccer? We're all on the same soccer team."

The saleswoman broke out into a big grin. "I have just the thing," she said. She opened a glass display case and pulled out a sterling silver link bracelet. She held it up, and dangling from it was a soccer ball charm dotted with tiny diamond accents. "It's our soccer charm bracelet," she said. "What do you think?"

We all looked at one another, speechless for a second as we stood with our mouths wide open and our eyes shining.

"It's perfect!" Frida finally gasped.

Emma smiled. "It was made for Zoe!"

"She'll always remember who it came from," Jessi added, beaming.

"How much is it?" I asked, nervous it would be too expensive. But the saleswoman named the price, and it was totally within our budget.

"We'll take it!" I cried.

"Would you like it gift wrapped?" she asked.

I looked at the other girls, who nodded. "Why not?" Jessi said.

As the saleswoman wrapped up the charm bracelet for us, I felt so happy. We had found the perfect gift for Zoe. I hoped finding the bracelet would work as a lucky charm for me, and that the *Kentville Chronicle* would print my letter soon!

CHAPTER fifteen

"Did they print it? Did they?" I barreled into the kitchen on Wednesday morning. I'd woken up and thrown on my school clothes before racing out of my bedroom and down the stairs. I had done the same thing the morning before, but no luck. The *Chronicle* hadn't printed my letter on Tuesday. So I was really, really hoping it would be in Wednesday's paper.

I crashed into Maisie, who was fully dressed and standing by the kitchen doorway holding a cup of orange juice. *Bam!* The juice flew up into the air, soaking both me and Maisie before the cup clattered to the floor.

"Mom!" Maisie cried, her face red. "Look what Devin did! I'm all wet, and it's her fault!"

Mom sat at the kitchen table, the newspaper spread out in front of her. My dad was at the kitchen counter, making Maisie's lunch. My mom sighed loudly and looked up from the paper.

"Maisie, I told you not to walk around the kitchen with your cup of juice. Sit at the table and drink it," Mom said firmly. "And, Devin, didn't I tell you yesterday not to race around the house? This isn't the soccer field."

"Sorry," I mumbled, feeling my hands getting all sticky from the orange juice. "I'll clean it up."

"I've got it," my dad said as he grabbed the mop from the kitchen closet. "Cleanup on aisle five!"

"Both of you, upstairs and change. And don't forget to wash your hands," Mom said.

"But what about the paper?" I asked.

"You'll find out after you've cleaned up," Mom said. "And only if you can walk into the kitchen, not run."

"Okay, got it," I said as I left the kitchen, forcing my legs not to race up the stairs.

Maisie followed me. She stuck out her tongue at me as we walked up the stairs. "Ha! You got in trouble."

I frowned at her. "So did you."

"It was your fault!" Maisie had that whiny tone to her voice that I knew from experience meant she wouldn't shut up about it. So I ignored her, walked into my room, and shut the door so I could change in peace. I heard her continue to grumble in the hallway before she stomped off to her own room.

I was a sticky OJ monster. Even my feet and pink flip-flops had gotten a soaking. I needed to wash them and change my shoes. Before I did that, I took a quick picture of myself with my cell phone and sent it to Kara.

Denim capris, striped tank complete with Maisie's OJ! When I ttyl I'll tell u the entire story!

When I lived in Connecticut, Kara and I used to pick out together what we would wear to school. Since I'd moved to California, with the three-hour time difference, we couldn't call each other in the mornings anymore. But we still texted each other pics of what we were wearing.

I washed off and threw on some clean clothes, including a new pair of flip-flops (red this time), and forced myself to walk slowly down the stairs and into the kitchen.

"Do-over?" I asked my mom, who was still sitting at the kitchen table. Thankfully, Maisie was still upstairs changing.

"Yes." Mom smiled at me. "And thanks for walking into the kitchen this time."

"Sure," I said. I sat down in the chair next to her. "So, is my letter in the paper?"

My mom nodded and grinned. "It sure is, and they printed it word for word. No misquotes this time."

She handed me the sports section. My eyes eagerly scanned the page until I found the letter. I quickly read it. It was exactly as I'd sent it. Whew! Now I had to hope that the other Kicks, especially the eighth graders, would read it.

I hurried to the practice field after school that day, worried I'd be late. Letter or not, the other Kicks would not be happy about that. Coach Valentine did not tolerate tardiness. But it totally wasn't my fault. My locker got stuck, and it took me forever to get it open.

I ran panting onto the field, fearing the worst. But it was strangely quiet. There was no sound of Coach Valentine's whistle or his gruff voice.

"He's late!" Jessi raced over to me while she rubbed her hands together, an evil gleam in her eyes. "I'm going to make him run laps. And do push-ups!"

I glanced up and saw everyone else on the team huddled together. I looked at Jessi with a raised eyebrow. "What's up?"

"They're reading today's paper," Jessi said. "More important, they are reading your letter in today's paper. Nice job, Devin."

I saw that Grace was in the center of the group, holding the newspaper.

"Sincerely, Devin Burke," I heard her say. She had been reading it out loud to the entire team!

I felt myself suck in a big gulp of air. Would they somehow find a way to get mad at me again?

Grace gave me a small smile. I took it as an invitation and walked over to her.

"Can we talk?" I asked.

"Okay," she said. We walked over to the edge of the field together.

"I just want you to know I meant every word I said in that letter," I told her.

Grace nodded slowly. "I liked that part about our team being like a family. Families sometimes fight. You should see the way I fight with my brother sometimes."

I nodded back. "Yeah. I just had a fight with my little sister this morning."

Grace sighed. "You know, Devin, that quote in the first newspaper article really hurt my feelings. You're not the only new person to the team. All of the seventh graders are. Us eighth graders, we played together last year, and we won only one game. And that was because of a forfeit! It was awful. We got teased a lot, especially by some of the boys on the soccer team."

I grimaced. I remembered how earlier in the season some of those boys, not Steven and Cody, had called us losers.

Grace continued. "It was really tough, but it brought all of us eighth graders closer, you know? After this year is over, we're moving on to high school. It's our last year on the Kicks. We're finally playing our best. And to have people think all the credit should go to the new blood, the seventh graders, hurts."

Aha! The eighth-grade resentment toward the seventh graders made a lot more sense to me now. I couldn't believe I hadn't thought of it before.

"So next year, you'll all still be Kicks," Grace added sadly. "At the very least, you'll be league championship Kicks, maybe even more before this season is done. But we'll be gone."

"All of us together will always be league championship Kicks!" I said. "We wouldn't be champions if it weren't for all of you. We did it as a team." And I meant it.

Grace gave me a small smile. "I just wanted you to know where we were coming from. That first newspaper article kicked up a lot of feelings." She laughed. "No pun intended. Coach Valentine would have loved that one."

I nodded. I understood, but I wished Grace had told me that from the beginning. We might have been able to work things out together as a team.

"That's why at the championship game, we wanted to do it all ourselves, so no one could say that we'd won because of you or the other seventh graders." Grace shook her head. "Now we all know what a bad idea that was."

"Yeah," I agreed. "But you saw it wasn't working, and we managed to win. All of us, the seventh and eighth graders together, as a team."

Grace nodded before looking over at the field. "Wow, Coach Valentine is still not here. We should start the warm-up," she said.

I smiled. "You do it, as the eighth-grade captain."

Grace returned my smile before walking back toward the Kicks, who were standing around chatting. "While we're waiting for Coach Valentine, let's warm up."

I joined them as the team began to run a lap around the field. But we didn't get far before a shrill scream pierced the air.

"Ahhhhhhhhhhh!"

The noise was coming from Emma. She had stopped in her tracks and was pointing across the field. A huge smile filled her face.

I looked in the direction where she was pointing. I saw a short woman with curly brown hair in the distance. She was wearing a familiar blue hoodie. It was Coach Flores!

"Coach!" I yelled.

Coach Flores smiled and waved. In one motion the Kicks turned and began running straight toward her, screaming and cheering as they ran.

As we got closer, I could see Coach Flores's eyes widen in mock fear. She held up her hands to block us. "It's a Kicks stampede!" she joked.

We jumped all over her anyway, practically knocking her over as everyone hugged her, talking the entire time.

"I missed you so much!" Zoe cried.

"It's great to have you back, Coach," Grace told her.

"Never, ever leave us again," Frida wailed. "It was horrible."

Coach Flores just laughed at that. "I don't think it was too horrible. You beat the Panthers. Congrats!"

Everyone began talking excitedly about the game. "And we had a shoot-out and everything!" Emma explained. "Hey, how is your dad doing?"

"I'm happy to say he's doing much better, and I'm so glad to be back here with my girls!" Coach Flores said, smiling. "We could chitchat all day, but we've got a big game coming up on Saturday. We better get to work! I want to see if Coach Valentine taught you any new tricks."

"I don't know about that, but he sure gave me some new *tics*," Frida said while she twitched her eye. Everyone started laughing at that, except Coach Flores, who kept a straight face, but I could tell she thought it was pretty funny.

"He was tough, even though sometimes he was kind of funny," Maya said. "But we really did miss you—a lot!"

"Let's spend some quality time on the soccer field, then," Coach Flores replied, grinning. "Count off for scrimmage!"

"It's like everything is coming together!" I told Kara that night during our video chat.

"So, did the eighth graders seem any different after reading the article and after your talk with Grace?" Kara asked.

I nodded. "When we played a scrimmage, I was on a team with Grace, Jade, Anjali, and Zarine. It felt like things were better, especially with Coach Flores there. Fingers crossed!" I held up my right hand and crossed my middle and index finger, and while I did that I crossed my eyes, too. It always made Kara laugh.

"Ha!" Kara giggled. "Are you ready for the regional game on Saturday?"

"We've got two more practices, so that will help," I said, but then I hesitated. The Cosmos had lost their last game and were out of the play-offs. I didn't want to make Kara feel bad. "But we don't have to talk about it."

Kara just laughed. "Don't worry about me, Devin. Yeah, it stinks that we're out of the play-offs, but we had a great season. Now I can put all my play-off hopes and dreams on you. I'm counting on you, Devin!" she said teasingly. "Do it for both of us!"

Just one of the million reasons I loved Kara. She was the best!

CHAPTER SIXTEEN

"This is crazy!" Jessi said as we walked into the gym on Friday afternoon.

The entire population of Kentville Middle School was climbing into the bleachers. Principal Gallegos stood in front of the crowd, holding a microphone. The school cheerleaders, dressed in blue and white, were warming up on the sidelines. A huge banner, painted by the sixth-period art class, hung from the gym wall. It had a picture of a kangaroo on it kicking a soccer ball, and the words, "Go, Kangaroos!"

"All right, girls. Let's line up over here," Coach Flores said, motioning to all of the Kicks. She was wearing a blue-and-white tracksuit that matched our uniforms, which we had worn to school that day.

"Good afternoon, students!" Principal Gallegos said in his usual loud voice. "I am so proud of our girls' soccer team today. Tomorrow our very own Kentville Kangaroos—otherwise known as the Kicks—will play their first game in the state championship tournament. Let's send them off with a big Kentville cheer!"

Everyone clapped, and I even heard a few high-pitched whistles. Then I heard the sound of a drumbeat, and the middle school marching band marched in, playing a really upbeat song. They weren't in full uniform, but they each wore blue jeans and a blue Kangaroos T-shirt, so the effect was still pretty awesome.

After the band finished, the cheerleaders did a routine, and they even made a pyramid. Emma nudged me.

"I still can't believe that this is all for us!" she said, her eyes wide.

"I know," I whispered back. "It's pretty awesome."

Principal Gallegos got back in front of the crowd. "Wasn't that great?" he asked. "And now I'd like to introduce Coach Flores."

Coach Flores looked at us. "Just like we practiced, okay?"

We all nodded as she picked up a soccer ball and jogged up to Principal Gallegos and took the microphone from him.

"Hey, everyone!" she began, and a bunch of kids clapped. "I'm so proud to be standing here today with the Kentville Kangaroos girls' soccer team. These girls worked hard this season to get where they are! And now I am proud to introduce . . . the Kicks!"

Grace was at the head of the line, and she jogged out onto the gym floor. We lined up along the back of the gym. Coach Flores put down the soccer ball and kicked it to Grace.

"First up, our eighth-grade captain . . . Grace Kirkland!"

Grace dribbled the ball across the gym and stopped next to Coach Flores. Then she turned and kicked the ball to the next girl in line.

"Next up is Megan Nowak!" Coach announced.

Megan dribbled the ball across the gym next, and then she kicked it to the next girl in line. It kept going like that until Jade, the last eighth grader, was introduced. It was my turn next, and I realized that my palms were really sweaty. I knew it was just a pep rally, but suddenly I felt as nervous as if I were playing in a game!

"Let's hear it for our seventh-grade captain, Devin Burke!"

I stopped the ball with my foot and started to dribble across the floor. I couldn't look up at the crowd, so I stared at my feet—which was a mistake. I lost my rhythm and tripped over my own left foot. The ball escaped from me, and I jogged after it, my face turning bright red. I could hear a few people laugh in the bleachers.

"Go, Devin!" Emma cheered, and in a flash I remembered how many times Emma had done embarrassing stuff like trip and fall on the field. Once, she had even kicked the ball into the wrong goal! But she never let it get to her. She always kept going.

I felt the heat leave my face as I smoothly dribbled the ball down to Coach. Then I turned and kicked it to Emma with a grateful smile.

Emma made it across the gym without even tripping once! One by one Coach Flores called out all my friends: Jessi, Zoe, Frida, Brianna, Sarah, Anna, and Olivia. I made sure to cheer extra loud for each of them.

"The Kicks wanted to say a special thank-you to Coach Valentine for getting the team through the play-offs. Stand up, Coach!"

Coach Valentine sat in the first row of bleachers, surrounded by the boys' team. He reluctantly stood up as his team chanted, "Coach! Coach! Coach!"

As planned, Grace and I took the microphone.

"Hey, Coach Valentine, we've got a question for you," Grace said. "Why did the soccer field get all wet?"

Coach laughed as he shrugged his shoulders.

"Because the soccer players dribbled all over it!" I said into the microphone.

Coach Valentine started laughing his signature loud, gruff laugh. All of the Kicks starting cracking up, as well as most of the boys' team.

"Thanks for helping us out when Coach Flores was gone," I added. "We'll miss you."

"But we won't miss the extra laps and push-ups," Grace joked.

Coach Valentine continued to laugh while giving us a thumbs-up.

Coach Flores took the microphone back. "And, of course, the boys' team had a great season too," she said. "Let's hear it for the boys!"

Everybody clapped and cheered for the boys, and the Kicks cheered for them extra hard. Cody jumped up and smiled and waved at everybody, but I noticed that some of the boys looked kind of miserable. A few, like this eighth grader named Trey Bishop, didn't even stand up. Trey had his hands folded across his chest, like he was angry or something.

I couldn't dwell on that, though, because then the band played another song, and we all just kind of danced around and clapped along to the music, and it was wonderful and amazing and crazy, and I got totally psyched up for the game.

Jessi high-fived me. "We are going to dominate the Bolts tomorrow!"

"Dominate!" I echoed.

The band's song ended just as the final bell of the day rang.

"Have a great weekend, everybody, and I hope to see you all in Brightville for the big game!" Principal Gallegos called out.

Kids poured out of the stands. Frida's drama club friends ran up and hugged her, and Jessi nudged me and nodded toward Cody and Steven, who were coming toward us.

In a panic I tried to secretly check my armpits because of how nervous I'd been before. When I looked back up,

Trey and a couple of the other eighth-grade players from the boys' team had sprung ahead of Cody and Steven. I was kind of surprised to see Trey right in my face.

"Nice move out there, Devin," Trey said. "If you kick like that on the field, you guys will do great."

The boys behind him snickered, but I didn't let it get to me.

"Whatever," I said, turning my back to them to face Jessi. She looked pretty angry.

But Trey didn't give up. "The only reason you guys won the play-offs is because you had *our* coach," he said.

I spun around. Now Trey wasn't just insulting me—he was insulting my team, and my coach. But before I could say anything, Grace, Megan, and Taylor were suddenly all over him.

"Back off, Trey," Megan said.

Trey shrugged. "It's true. Coach Valentine is the only reason you guys won."

"Oh, yeah?" Taylor asked. "Then why didn't *you* guys win?"

That shut Trey up—for a second. "Yeah, well, Devin can't kick anyway. Did you see her out there? She tripped over her own feet." Then he did an impression that was supposed to be me tripping, but he looked totally stupid (and I know my mom and dad taught me never to use that word, but trust me, it was the best word to describe Trey at that moment).

"Devin's a great player," Grace said in her usual chill

voice. "And I'm pretty sure she's better than you."

Trey looked like he was going to say something, but then Cody tapped him on the shoulder. "Um, I think Coach wants to talk to you."

Trey looked over at Coach Valentine, who looked pretty mad. I swear that Trey turned a little pale as he slipped off to face his coach.

I looked at Grace. "Hey, thanks," I said.

Grace smiled at me. "No problem. He's such a jerk sometimes."

That was the moment when I knew that things were okay with me and Grace. Like, really okay. I knew one more thing for sure: if we lost to the Bolts the next day, it wouldn't be because we weren't working as a team.

If Grace would stick up for me to Trey, I knew she'd have my back on the soccer field. And if Megan and Taylor would too, I knew they'd treat the other seventh graders the same. The Kicks had the skills. Now all we needed was the teamwork, and the state championships would be within our reach!

CHAPTER SEVENTEEN

My stomach did flip-flops during the whole drive to Brightville the next morning. I was excited and nervous at the same time. I was confident that we were going to win, and terrified that we were going to lose. It reminded me of when my mom would tell me, "Your emotions are all over the place!"

Part of it was that I hadn't been able to talk to Kara that morning, because she had play practice. It also didn't help that Maisie insisted on singing along with the radio station. I put my earbuds in so that I could listen to my own music, but Maisie was so loud that I could still hear her.

I took out one earbud. "Mom, could you please ask her to stop?" I asked.

Mom sighed. "You can ask her yourself, Devin."

"But she won't listen to me," I protested. Maisie was

singing that whole time, so she could have stopped then if she'd wanted to. But of course she didn't.

"You two need to learn how to communicate with each other," Mom said. "This family is a team too, you know."

When she put it like that, I couldn't argue. So I gave it my best shot.

I turned to my little sister. "Maisie, can you please stop singing?"

She stopped long enough to answer. "But it's my favorite song!"

Mom was watching in the rearview mirror, and I rolled my eyes at her, but she didn't say anything.

I tried another tactic. "Maisie, here's the thing. I'm really nervous about the game, okay? And it would really help if you stopped singing now. I swear you can sing the whole way back and I won't say anything."

Maisie stopped. "Promise?"

"Promise," I said, nodding solemnly.

"Okay," Maisie said. Then she started silently mouthing the words to the song, and I gratefully put my earbuds back in. Mom grinned into the mirror.

"See what a little teamwork can do?" she asked.

I turned my music back on and stared out the window. Would teamwork be enough for the Kicks to beat the Bolts? I would find out soon enough.

It was a familiar scene when we pulled into the parking lot—lots of balloons and signs in yellow and white, the Bolts' colors, and fans wearing Bolts yellow. I wasn't intimidated by that anymore, but then I saw the Bolts warming up on the field.

Their coach had them dribbling through cones, and they were sailing through the course really fast, and really smoothly. I stood at the edge of the field for a few seconds, watching. Not one of them lost control of the ball, even for a second.

Frida and Zoe stepped up next to me.

"They're really tall," Zoe remarked anxiously. Since she only came up to about my shoulders, I could understand why she was worried.

"And fast," Frida added. She looked a little pale.

I couldn't let my teammates get psyched out. "Remember, the Panthers looked pretty impressive the first time we saw them, too. And we ended up beating them twice."

Zoe nodded. "You're right," she said. "But I'm starting to feel stage fright again."

"You're going to do great," Frida assured her.

"Do you have a character yet for the game?" I asked Frida.

"Well, I was thinking of one," she said, still staring at the Bolts. "But now I'm thinking I might be Invisible Girl."

Then Emma and Jessi joined us.

"No way should you be invisible!" Jessi said.

"Yeah," Emma agreed.

"But I'm scared of those Bolts," Frida said with a shiver.

"Then go big," Jessi urged. "Like . . . Godzilla."

"*Mega*-Godzilla!" Emma added.

A slow grin came over Frida's face. "Yeah, being a giant monster might be just the thing. . . ."

"Come on," I said. "Let's warm up."

We joined the rest of the team, and Coach Flores led us in warm-ups. We did our sock swap, as always, and then it was almost game time. My butterflies came back big-time.

Then I heard a call from the stands. "Devin!"

I turned and saw Steven there, sitting next to Cody. I couldn't believe it! They had come all the way to Brightville for the game. I tapped Jessi on the shoulder, and her face lit up as she looked into the stands.

Then I saw my mom come running up to the sidelines, motioning to me. I jogged up to her.

"What is it?" I asked.

She held out her phone. "Somebody wants to wish you luck."

I looked down and saw Kara's face on the screen and let out a scream.

"Kara!"

"I just got back," she said. "I know your game's about to start. I'll be thinking of you the whole time, okay?"

"Okay," I said, and then I heard Coach Flores calling the team onto the field. "Gotta run!"

My butterflies disappeared as I ran out to take my place on the field. Seeing Steven and Kara had given me the extra boost that I needed. When the starting whistle blew, I was ready for anything.

After a few seconds I found out that the Bolts lived up to their name. They had control of the ball and they tore down the field like lightning.

But we were ready for them. Our midfielders kept pace with their offense, keeping close to them. Grace even stole the ball right out from under one of the Bolts forwards, but another player swept up and got it right back from her. The Bolts player charged the goal and lobbed a kick, but Emma caught it before it could go in.

That's how it went for most of the first half. Anytime we got control of the ball, one of the Bolts ran up in a blur and stole it from us. Emma did a great job of protecting the goal, but on the Bolts' fifth attempt one of their strikers kicked a ball that whizzed right over her head, and the Bolts were up, 1–0.

"Sorry!" Emma called out.

"Don't worry. You're doing great!" I called back—and Grace yelled the same thing at the same time. We looked at each other and smiled.

No matter how hard we tried, we couldn't score at all in the first half—and the Bolts got another one past Emma, bringing the score to 2–0. Coach Flores gave us a pep talk at halftime.

"Listen, I know those Bolts are fast, but you girls are doing your best out there, and I'm proud of you," she said.

"Keep doing what you're doing. I can't ask for any more."

I knew coach wasn't just being nice—she was right. Everybody was playing their heart out. But I was starting to worry that our best wasn't going to be good enough.

Coach switched out some players and put Zarine in for Emma on goal. I had my hopes up when the second half started and Zoe got control of the ball. She was the fastest on our team, and her lightning moves had never failed to confuse our opposition.

But the Bolts defense was just as fast. Zoe made her way down the field, turning left, then right, then faking a left and going straight. She tried every trick she knew, but she couldn't shake the Bolts defense.

Finally we got a break. One of the Bolts got the ball away from Zoe, but the kick went a little wild. Grace rescued it and sent it soaring toward the goal. The goalie dove for it but missed. We had scored!

I high-fived Grace and got ready for the throw-in. The score was Bolts 2, Kicks 1. That was something we could work with.

But Grace's goal seemed to light the Bolts on fire too. The goalie threw the ball to one of the Bolts players, and she rocketed down the side of the field. We chased after her but couldn't catch up.

"Rooooooooaaar!" Frida raced up and kicked the ball away from her, growling like some kind of crazed beast.

"All right, Frida!" I yelled as Maya ran up to the ball— but one of the Bolts, who had been keeping pace with her teammate, swooped in and stole it. She took it right up to the goal and kicked it past Zarine. The Bolts had scored again!

I ran up to Grace.

"What are we going to do?" I asked. "We've got to confuse them somehow."

"I'm not sure," Grace admitted. "Let's stick together and keep passing."

I nodded. It was worth a try anyway, so Grace and I quickly passed the word on to the other players. Jade got control of the ball first, and we all kind of stuck with her as she dribbled up the middle. Then she passed it to Maya, who passed it to Taylor, who passed it to Grace—short, fast passes. The Bolts were all over us, but we managed to keep control of the ball.

When we got close to the goal, Jessi passed it to me. I quickly scanned the field for my options. Megan and Alandra were close by, but they were swarmed by defenders—and I had a clear shot at the goal.

I took it, aiming the ball a little to the left in the hopes of confusing the goalie a bit. The ball skidded across the grass, and for a second I worried that it would be too easy to stop. I held my breath as the goalie dove . . . and watched the ball slip right under her.

The Kicks fans went wild! We had scored again. Now it was Bolts 3, Kicks 2. I high-fived with a bunch of teammates and then tried to refocus for the rest of the game.

Just as they had when Grace had scored, the Bolts

came back with a vengeance. They forged down the field at superspeed, blasting past our defenders, and one of their strikers made another goal.

Now the score was 4–2, Bolts, and I suddenly got that feeling that you can get in a game, like there's no hope. It's a terrible feeling, and one that can't ever lead anywhere good. But it's a hard one to shake off, and I think my teammates had it as well.

Not that we gave up—we didn't. But we just couldn't get past their defenders again. Coach put Emma in the goal for the last stretch, and she stopped two more goal attempts.

I wish I could say that we scored two more goals, and then at the last second I scored the winning goal and we won by one point. But what happened was a lot more boring—and a lot sadder—than that. I was running down the field, getting ready to accept a pass from Taylor, when the ref's whistle blew.

Somebody went offsides, I thought, but then I saw the Bolts jumping up and hugging one another and cheering, followed by a deafening sound from the Bolts' stands. That's when it hit me—the Bolts had won, and we had lost.

We hadn't lost a game in weeks, and it was almost like I'd forgotten what it felt like. It was awful. Terrible. Not only had we lost the game, but we'd lost our chance to win the state championship—and this meant that our season was over too.

I felt a tap on my arm, and I saw Jessi standing next to me.

"Come on. We've got to shake hands with the Bolts," she said.

The other Kicks were walking up to the line of Bolts like zombies, and I'm sure I looked like a zombie too. Zoe had tears in her eyes, and when I saw that, I felt like crying.

When we got back to the sidelines, Coach Flores was cheerful, as always.

"I am so proud of you guys!" she said. "You played a great game." She clapped and let out a "Whoop," hoping we would join her, but nobody said anything.

"All right, then. Let's get out of here," Coach said. "We've all got Zoe's bat mitzvah to get to!"

I looked at Zoe again, and now she was looking down at her sneakers. Emma put an arm around her.

"Don't worry. It's going to be a great party," she said, but for once Emma's optimism didn't rub off on me.

We had lost the game. Our season was over. I really didn't feel like going to a party—and I'm sure the rest of the Kicks didn't either.

CHAPTER EIGHTEEN

"Devin, you look beautiful! Twirl around again!" Kara demanded.

I twirled around in my blue dress in front of my computer screen. I had showered and changed as soon as we'd gotten home, and I had promised Kara that she could see the final result.

"Oh my gosh, you're gorgeous!" she said. "So why don't you look happy?"

"You know why," I said. "We lost! The season is over."

"Yeah, but you're in California, and they have soccer programs all year long," Kara pointed out. "I have to wait until March for spring soccer. Besides, you won your league! The Cosmos didn't even do that."

"I know," I said with a sigh. "It's just . . . losing stinks."

"Everybody loses sometimes, Devin," she said. "Even super-amazing professionals. It's part of the sport."

"Why do you always have to be right?" I teased.

"Because I am perfect!" Kara said. "Now get out of here and go have a good time, you weirdo!"

I stuck my tongue out at her and shut down the laptop. Then I hurried down the stairs, glad that my mom had bought me some sparkly silver flats to wear with the dress.

"You look nice," my dad said when he saw me.

"So do you," I said. Dad wore a navy-blue suit with a light blue shirt and a red tie. Then I looked at Mom and Maisie. Mom had on a navy-blue dress with short sleeves, and Maisie had on a blue dress the same color as mine.

"Oh my gosh, we're the crazy matching family!" I cried.

"Blue is a very popular color," Mom said. "Anyway, we all look wonderful."

Dad looked at his watch. "Come on. We don't want to be late!"

As we drove to the temple, I could feel my disappointment about losing start to lift a little. It lifted even more when we got inside. The temple room was really beautiful, with gleaming wood benches and stained glass.

I quickly spotted Jessi and Emma, and we went to sit with them. Jessi's mom and dad were there, and so were Emma's parents.

"Oh my gosh, you guys look great!" I told Jessi and Emma. I looked down at Emma's feet and saw that she had on sparkly flats too. I stuck out my right foot so that Emma could see that we matched.

Emma grinned. "Nice."

Frida and her mom rushed in next, and Frida looked totally gorgeous too. She had her wavy auburn hair held back in a black sequined headband that matched her dress.

"Are we late?" Frida asked.

"I think it's about to start," I said.

Then Zoe walked in, followed by her parents and all three of her older sisters. She gave us a little wave and a smile as she walked past.

"She picked the black-and-white dress," Jessi whispered to me.

I nodded. "She looks awesome!"

I had never been to a bat mitzvah service before, so I didn't know what to expect. It ended up being really beautiful. The rabbi played this totally mellow music on a guitar, and Zoe's sister Jayne sang a beautiful song, and Zoe had to do this whole speech in front of everybody, and she didn't even sound nervous! I was really impressed.

When the service was over, Zoe was superhappy and practically jumping out of her heels.

"The party is upstairs, everybody!" she announced.

We all followed her directions to the second floor of the temple, which was this huge room with lots of windows. The red carpet led from the entrance into the party room.

"Oh my gosh, it's beautiful!" Emma exclaimed when we stepped inside.

The room was decorated with black-and-white bal-loons and streamers. Each table was set with either a black or a white tablecloth, and each place was set with the black-and-white favors we'd made. In the center of each table was a big collage with pictures of models in different outfits, with a name sprawled across each collage.

Zoe ran up and grabbed me by the arm.

"Each table is named after one of my favorite designers," she said. "You guys are at the Betsey Johnson table. Come on!"

Jessi, Emma, and Frida followed as Zoe dragged me across the room to a big, round table near the deejay booth.

"I've got to go do some stuff," she said. "I have to sit with my family, but I'll squeeze in with you guys later, promise."

Zoe sped off, and we took our seats. Brianna, Sarah, Anna, and Olivia came and joined us. Jessi nodded to the two empty seats left at the table.

"I wonder who's sitting there," she said.

That's when I looked up and saw Cody and Steven standing there, grinning.

"Is this the Betsey Johnson table?" Cody asked.

"You bet," Jessi said with a grin.

I looked across the room and caught Zoe's eye. She winked at me, and I knew she had set this up.

"I didn't know you guys were coming," I said as the boys sat down. Steven had on a short-sleeved light blue shirt and a dark blue tie, and I couldn't help thinking how nice he looked.

"Yeah, Zoe invited a bunch of us from school," Cody said.

"I've known her since kindergarten," Steven added.

Over at the deejay table a guy wearing a tux grabbed the microphone.

"All right," Cody said. "Let's get this party started!"

"Welcome, everyone, to Zoe's bat mitzvah!" the deejay announced. "Now let's hear a nice warm welcome for Zoe's family! First up, her sisters, Opal, Jayne, and Yvette!"

Zoe's sisters walked in on the red carpet, and everybody clapped and cheered. Then the deejay introduced her mom and dad, and finally . . .

"Miss Zoe Amelia Quinlan!" the deejay said.

Everyone at our table stood up and started whooping and hollering like crazy. Zoe looked totally gorgeous and poised as she walked down the red carpet. Then she made her way up to the deejay booth and stopped at a small, round table set with unlit white candles. The deejay handed her the microphone.

"Thanks for coming, everybody," Zoe said a little shyly. "Before we start everything, there are a few people I want to thank."

She took a deep breath as she unfolded a piece of paper she'd been carrying.

"You always cheer me up when I feel sad. I love you so much, Mom and Dad."

Mr. and Mrs. Quinlan walked up to the table, and together they lit one of the candles with Zoe. She gave them both a big hug.

"Oh, that's so sweet!" Emma said.

Zoe read more rhymes for all the different people in her life—her sisters, her aunt and uncle, and her cousins. Then she smiled and looked over at us.

"Win or lose, they're all great chicks. This candle is for all of the Kicks!" she said.

Nervous and giggling, all eighteen of us approached Zoe and tried our best to put one hand each on the candle lighter. We were all squished together, but we did it. Then Zoe handed the microphone back to the deejay.

"Okay. Zoe wants this dance for the Kicks! Coach Flores, you get up here too!" he said.

Then the music was blaring, and we all started dancing and jumping around. Coach Flores started doing this thing where she was jabbing her arms, like she was boxing.

"Yo, Coach! Busting out the moves!" Jessi yelled, and we all cracked up.

Zoe grabbed Emma's hand, and they twirled around, which was funny because Zoe was so short and Emma was so tall. Frida was spinning around and waving her arms, and the fringe on her dress swung back and forth. Jessi faced me and started jumping up and down, and I jumped with her.

I didn't feel like a loser anymore. Not even a little bit. After all, I had my friends around me, and my whole team.

As long as I had them, I knew I would always be a winner!